SEAMSTRESS

David Mercaldo, Ph.D.

CROWN OAK PRESS

*For my wife Linda, who is a constant source
of encouragement to me… and in loving memory of my mother,
Rose Giangola Mercaldo, who bore seven children,
and also" did a little sewing on the side!"*

Foreword

Once upon a time there was a woman who worked in the garment
industry as a SEAMSTRESS. For 10 to 12 hours a day she sat
in front of a sewing machine and earned a few dollars to help
support her family. She lived a simple life and considered her
place - an honorable station amidst a vast army of workers in
the mid twentieth century. Like the garments she sewed, the
SEAMSTRESS came in many shapes, sizes and colors. She was
16 years old or 50! And who was this woman? We knew her as
grandma, mom, sister, aunt, cousin, wife and friend. She is part of
the greatness that is America and with this novel I salute each of
them and keep their memory alive now…and forevermore!
-and to the 146 women who gave their lives at the
ill-famed Triangle Shirt Waist Factory…
we will never forget you!

The Enrico Caruso Museum of America

Cav. Uff. Aldo H. Mancusi
1942 East 19th Street
Brooklyn, N.Y. 11229

Museum Phone/Fax
(718)368-3993

Email Address
CarusoMuseumNY@aol.com

www.enricocarusomuseum.com

Thank you, David Mercaldo, for the skillful way you portrayed this wonderful story of Italian immigrant families in America! As we look over our shoulders at the not too distant past, we are literally educated by these pages as to how life really was when family and friends were most important. The friendship and love of life depicted in this book showed how people were brought together and remained friends for a lifetime.

Once you begin to read this book you won't put it down because it parallels many aspects of our life today. Santina Fortunato, a SEAMSTRESS - was a woman with only an eighth grade education, yet she shows herself to be a genius in many ways as we see her resolve the difficult problems of her friends and family. With her boundless love and concern for others she brings a wealth of wisdom to the lives of those she comes in contact with during her lifetime.

Indeed, Santina Fortunato ("fortunate" in English), was 'fortunate' in many ways to have such a wonderful family and dedicated friends. We are also fortunate to have this book as it brings a sense of pride in the accomplishments of our ancestors. This book should be a must read for all adults and especially students as it gives us an historical view of the struggles of immigrant parents and what they went through to give us a better life.

Thank you, David, for allowing me the privilege of reading this book before publication. I am the son of Italian immigrant parents and can say this book brought tears to my eyes and joy to my heart! Yes...thank you!

CAVALIERE UAFFICIALE ALDO MANCUSI PRES.
THE ENRICO CARUSO MUSEUM OF AMERICA

CONTENTS

SEAMSTRESS

Part One

S antina Fortunato picked up the STATEN ISLAND ADVANCE as she did each morning and thumbed the pages until she reached the obituary section. Reading the obituaries had become a daily ritual in her search for memories long past. Within the lines of the death notices were precious jewels of information that reflected on the times and places of long ago…of friends and neighbors who adorned her life.

She knew that someday her own epitaph would appear and hoped her family and friends would think back to the days when she was young. Those were the days she wished they would remember… fleeting moments of youth, fantasy and innocence. Surely the early days in ones life were forever captured in the memory of her peers. She imagined that in heaven, everyone was twenty-five years old. That is, except for the "old people!" They were never really young she thought…they were too old to be young. She could not imagine these people at age twenty or thirty because she first came to know them when they were fifty years and older. And, after all, they were supposed to be old.

She wanted to be remembered for the early days…days of care-free living and loving; but she also wanted to be remembered for her profession. She was a daughter, wife, mother, aunt, grandmother and now great–grandmother; yet she clung to the memories of the early days…when she ventured from her eighth grade graduation ceremony to the real world…the world of work.

"Signora Santina Fortunato," as they would call her at her funeral, would also die someday and the paper would record her passing.

She considered herself an insignificant player in a mid twentieth century city landscape. The daughter of Italian immigrants, Santina had no great exploits attached to her name. She had lived a simple life…unassuming and uneventful; like her people before had lived in the old country. Her offspring thought otherwise. They saw beyond the simplicity of a sweet girl growing up in, what they imagined was, an uncomplicated world and were fascinated with her endurance and tenacity. They promised to reveal all of her notable accomplishments in her epitaph, but she would smile at them and counter.

"No, no, my dear children it must read..."*Santina Fortunato...*
SEAMSTRESS! "

Of late, the obituary page accounted for the death of several friends from the old neighborhood in Rosebank, a little hamlet on Staten Island. Their death notices and pictures evoked fond memories of a time when life was uncomplicated and promising.

The obituary column announced the passing of her friend Angelina Caruso. The details of her death notice were preceded by one word that was highlighted in bold type under her name..."HOMEMAKER." Of course, Santina must pay her respects, having known the woman for so many years. It was more than an obligation…it was her duty!

In the late afternoon, she would make her way to the Azzara Funeral Home on Sand Lane in South Beach. There, she would meet her other friends and for a few hours they would reminisce about the old days. This is what they did each time they met and tonight, in the witness of the dead, they would detail the same stories and remind each other of the days when they all gathered in the upper loft of Harry and Isadore Neuremberg's Store - located in the heart of the garment district. They would retell the same stories and their laughter would be as intense as if they were hearing them for the first time. The intercourse was predictable; they would each take turns gossiping about the people they knew and had seen of late. It was nothing less than an inventory of the people who filled the years of their lives. Then each would report how their many grandchildren were doing, who moved and of course those who died. They had shared so much with so many people, that they could talk for hours on end.

But in spite of all the people they knew and the things that had happened in their lives, the days of working together in the crowded, impersonal sweatshop, somehow transcended all other memories. Then, they were part of an army...a workforce that labored so their children and grandchildren could have a *better life*!

In the early part of the century, dozens of small manufacturers crowded into the narrow buildings flanking the busy streets of lower Manhattan. The alleys were filled with vendors, scurrying merchants and racks of clothing being pushed or pulled from one store to another. It was like a world unto itself, with each store specializing in some phase of clothing manufacture or sale. The *Neuremberg Brothers* had inherited the business from their father and uncle. The sign covering the front of their building told the public that they were *clothiers*...specializing in design and manufacturing; but in truth, the brothers couldn't even hold a pair of scissors and their 'designing' was left to Aldo Mancini, an immigrant from Naples. Like most Italian craftsmen, the small-framed Mancini would live and die an unsung artisan, hidden beneath the stitches of the *Neuremberg Clothiers* label.

The small work area located on the second floor above the modest showroom, housed six industrial sewing machines, with bolts of fabric and supplies strewn about. One large table was used by Aldo to design, lay out and cut his patterns; while in front of the large window overlooking the busy streets, Santina and her girlfriends sat at their work stations and assembled the parts of each garment...ever sewing and chatting the day away.

There, in the dimly lit, impersonal and sparsely furnished loft, five young Italian women battled the heat and cold and lived together for forty to sixty hours a week. In this small industrial sanctuary sat Santina, Adelina Rocco, Antoinette Mancini, Josephina Mura, and Carmella Bruno. They would establish a bond that would last a lifetime.

Their travel routine to the store was as predicable as all of the practices that governed their lives. Rain or shine, four of the girls would meet at the subway station at Battery Park. Then they would walk twelve blocks to the store. Carmella, who lived in Manhattan, would be waiting for them on the corner. After a cordial greeting, the five would duck into Duffy's candy store and buy the required staples for a day at work...*Dentine, Sen Sen* and cigarettes. A small brown bag, neatly tucked away in their large purses, held the necessary food and snacks to keep them going during the long day. There were no two-martini lunches; like in the movies that they raced to each Saturday afternoon, because every penny they made was brought home to papa and mamma for the needs of their family. Upon exiting the candy store, they would see one of their bosses, Isadore, running up the street with his familiar awkward gate. Incorporated into his neurotic movements and the fumbling of a large ring of keys, was his mumbling...and did he mumble! Often the girls would hear voices in the bathroom or in one of the closets as if two people were arguing. It was usually Isadore, nervously chanting or discussing something with himself.

The doors to the small hallway, leading to the narrow steps which took them to their work room, were locked until he arrived. Never would he trust one of the girls to have an extra key to open the shop early. He would clumsily insert two or three keys before he found the correct one, then turn to his workers and bellow, "All right....all right...let's get started, girls!" With endearing tones and an arm around his shoulder, Adeline would purr directly into his ear in her native *Italian tongue...*"*Oh, Mr. Neuremberg, you're such an ugly cheapskate... we hate working for you and your miserable brother!*" By the time the girls reached the top step, they were laughing hysterically.

A few minutes later, when Brother Harry arrived, the block would echo with their yelling and arguing which continued until their first customer arrived. They hated each other, but vowed to remain partners until their mother died...shielding her from the reality of their mutual hatred. But things did not turn out according to their plans. She buried both of them, passing herself two weeks later while sitting on the toilet in the shop. What they didn't know is that she loathed their loathing and had made her own deal with God regarding the timing of her death.

On the street, one would never know that these same girls were seamstresses because they walked from their home to the shop in beautiful clothing...with fashionable ankle strapped pumps and a face full of the popular make-up of the day. But within a few minutes of their arrival at the shop, each would don a smock and kerchief and look like the tens of thousands of others who worked in the industry doing the same mundane tasks, day after day and year after year.

Yet, the memory of those days shone bright in Santina's mind and from time to time, she would relate little stories to her children and grandchildren. "Those were beautiful days," she would tell them, adding, "we were like sisters!" She perished the day she would stand over any of their graves. There was no reason for any of them to still be alive...to live beyond the days of their respective husbands...and in some cases, children. But they did, and lived out those years alone, clutching to the memories of long ago when they lived in what they remembered as a perfect world...ordered and easy. The girls had their share of health problems, but these paled in light of other things that had happened to them over the years. However, not everyone in their age group survived the darts of sickness and death!

Today, the funeral for Signora Caruso would be simple. The priest would tell everyone that she served her family and died honorably. Oh yes, he would say she was a "good woman!" This was important, because to the Italians, the highest honor a woman could be bestowed was the title, *GOOD WOMAN*. It meant that she was all that she should be...a loving daughter and sister, faithful wife, dedicated mother, loving aunt...with the heart of a servant! Oh yes, she would also be honored for being a daughter of the church. Her husband, Sal, had died ten years before when cancer moved slowly and methodically through his entire body until he expired one night in bed. Earlier in the week, Angelina suffered a fatal heart attack and left her children with nothing but memories, the legacy of a good family name and an old house in West Brighton.

Santina remembered the days of her youth when the *old people* sat and talked in the dining room while the cousins played in the parlor. Now Santina faced the reality that she and her peers had become..."*The Old People.*" Closing in on seventy-five years found her tired and more dependent. Now the days moved slowly forward one at a time. She had not been well herself during the past five years and now sugar diabetes stalked the good health of younger days. But she was alive and very much aware of the years. She could remember finite details of things that happened more than half a century before and when any member of the family wanted to know a date for a birth, wedding or death...they would call Zia Santina. She was their *memory* bank.

Her day passed quickly and she made contact with each of the girls to let them know she would be at the funeral parlor. All five agreed to eat at *Tung Bo Restaurant* after the wake and have "chinks." The obvious prejudice in their casual and caustic announcement to visit the local Chinese restaurant for supper was standard jargon among them. When they ordered, the table would be filled with an abundance of family style platters. It was part of their tradition...to taste a little of this and a little of that. When the check was paid, they would each go home with a brown bag or two of *left-over food*. And while each claimed the scraps would serve as lunch the next day, no one would betray the truth that their grandchildren would feast on the left-overs...that their taste buds no longer clamored for day old chop suey, but for food with less exotic spices.

On this particular day, her car was in the repair shop and not wanting to trouble anyone for a ride, she decided to take public transportation for the short trip. At four-thirty, Santina boarded the local bus, which headed down Bay Street. When it came to her stop, she pulled the chord and the bus slowly pulled to the curb at MacLean Ave. She stepped off the bus and began her walk to Azzara Funeral Home. For all of her years... public transportation chauffeured her throughout the Island and city when Vito used the car during the day for work. When he passed on, she kept the aging Dodge, using it just a few times a week to shop and visit. Now it was old and she had decided it was either time to use public transportation or buy a new car. She had put a deposit on one, just days before, but didn't know if she would go through with the deal or not.

When the children were young, her neighborhood provided all the necessary stores for food and clothing. For the most part, she walked everywhere.

In the early days, at six in the morning, she would board the Staten Island Ferry and glide across the waters at the mouth of the Hudson and on to her job. Antoinette, who also lived on the Island, traveled with her, while Josephina and Adeline lived in the Bensonhurst section of Brooklyn and rode a subway into Manhattan. Eventually, all of the girls moved to Staten Island and became neighbors, but for the few miles that separated their houses

A few minutes later she was at the funeral home. Santina could never figure out why funeral directors called it a "home," because no one lived there and without a kitchen...could it really be considered a home? She liked the words *funeral parlor* better, because she remembered the days when the dead were laid out in their homes... in the front parlor. She thought about the first time she had ever seen a body in a house for viewing. It was that of her grandmother, Tomasina Colegera Cerullo. The large framed woman appeared crowded in the pine box and to her granddaughter she appeared like a department store manikin...with bright red lipstick and rouge. She couldn't remember ever seeing her in such bawdy make-up and the old woman appeared like a stranger to her.

Over the years, out of duty and respect, she had made her vigil to honor the dead. In those days, there were just a few funerals; now it had become a regular activity for her family and friends.

Memories of the past were threaded with both joy and sorrow. In her heart, she sometimes pined for the past, resigning that she could not go back and redeem the years. Now it was her pleasure to spend time with her grandchildren and play games in her mind as to what would become of them in a world that seemed to do nothing else but change. She hoped they would remain innocent and sweet, gentle and loving...storing memories to be unlocked and viewed in the years to come...like she was doing now.

Her own first memory was that of her mother's kitchen and the sweet scent of oven-baked bread. She envisioned her mother kneading the dough as she watched from the high chair. She could not have been more than two years old, but that sight was as clear as if she had been twenty! She vividly remembered the simple flower-print housedress her mother wore as she pulled the dough back and forth, occasionally mashing it on the wooden board she used only for baking purposes. She still had the same wooden board and sometimes, when she took it out and began to knead flour, tears would fill her eyes.

Other kitchen utensils also had highly designated functions. The wooden stirring spoon, for instance, was not only used to stir the sauce, but was also used to stir the fanny when one of the children got out of line.

The sound of her mother working in the kitchen would beckon her grandmother, whom she knew as "Mamma-Nonna," to come down from her upstairs apartment. The two would work together to form the loaves. After all, the family was large and bread would be filling. The staples were red sauce, pasta, sausage and peppers. Oh yes, meatballs were on the menu too. And, of course, there were always family guests...invited or not!

At times, when Aunt Rose would visit, she would insist on making her famous meatballs. To do so, she would demand the kitchen and twenty minutes of solitude to boot! Santina's father would comment that they were all permitted to eat Rosie's meatballs on Friday... instead of the required fish, because there were more breadcrumbs and seasoning in the mix than meat. Memories of those times and the sweet taste of her meatballs still lingered after all these years.

Among her first memories, were those of her papa and the time she refused to eat her green beans. She remembered his stern and compelling voice when he demanded, "Inna thissa housa, we eata everytinga onna the plate!"

"And we all did...whether we liked it or not!" Santina would tell her family, years later.

The children never found out what would happen if they rebelled because each child knew to revere and obey all of the elders in the family...whether they were a year or fifty-years older. It was all part of the order in the Italian home.

Santina's childhood was simple and focused. Everyone had a job to do in the house and the children...well children were supposed to be children...obedient and respectful. Life had an uncomplicated road map. She would attend a public school until the eighth grade, then get a job and commute to the big city. While in her latter teen years or early twenties at the latest, she would be married. It was a pattern that her entire community accepted and followed. To be single in your mid-twenties meant that "something was wrong!"

Santina could still hear the next door neighbors explaining to her parents why their daughter Sophia wasn't married.

"She's a gooda girl, butta the boysa dona aska her outta!" they complained. Santina had her own thoughts about the girl they called *"Single Sophie!"*

Sophia was nearly three hundred pounds and really didn't look all that bad. After all, she was taller than her parents and looked rather imposing when they stood together; she stood exactly five foot four and one half inches with heels on! She remembered the day when Sophia announced she had met a boy and wanted to date him. Her father met the would-be Romeo at the door and asked him one question. "My daughter tella me you name isa Craig...you are Irish?" When the lad smiled and said he was, the door slowly closed on him and Sophia's only chance to meet a perspective husband. She ran up the stairs to her room in bitter tears and consoled herself by eating several boxes of chocolate malts. An hour later she emerged with a smile on her face and sat down to a big plate of spaghetti and meatballs. She never married.

For Santina, marrying Vito Fortunato was the best thing that ever happened to her. She met him at a street fair on September 5, 1931. It was a Friday night and the streets were crowded with people celebrating their patron saint, when Vito offered to buy her a zeppole. By Sunday afternoon she had introduced him to her father and mother... and three months later they were married. Vito was a painter and worked for a local construction company, Mc Henry & Son.

Following a macaroni dinner on that first Sunday after Mass, Santina's father turned to Vito and questioned him.

"You worka for the Irish?"

"They're good people Mr. Calabrese! I have no complaints," he respectfully responded.

"Somaday, you havva you owna bizziness, no?" The elder fired back.

"I'd like that, but it costs money...more than I have right now," Vito replied.

"How mucha money you needa for you to be onna you own?" The anxious father pressed.

"Well, I'd say about $250.00 for supplies, a ladder and brushes," he answered.

On the day of their wedding, the 'Old Man' took Vito aside and pressed a bundle of rolled bills into his hand and whispered.

"We dona worka for the Irish! You be you owna bossa and you taka gooda care of my Santina...capisce?

Within two weeks, Vito filed a business certificate and began his own company. He worked, never missing a day for nearly thirty years. Later, when they needed closing money for the purchase of their first house, again the family Patriarch questioned the family painter. "How mucha you needa for the closa?"

Seven hundred dollars was a inconceivable amount of money for a family to save in 1934, but again, the old man pressed a roll of bills into his hands and announced, "You taka gooda care ofa my Santina, capisce?"

When his daughter protested a few minutes after Vito showed her the money, her father raised his voice, "You dona tella you father whata to do! Vito is a gooda man and he willa taka care for you! You say to you father, *Thank you, Papa!*" With this, she clutched his neck and shoulders and cried..."I love you papa!" He gently pushed her away and spoke, "Thatsa better...now go to you husband!" Across the room her mother Lucia smiled with tears streaming down her face. When her father saw her mother crying, he announced to the family...."half hour," indicating Lucia was known for long bouts of joyful tears. Santina ran to her mother, crying, "Mamma!"

The celebration that followed that evening was a simple one. Mamma Nonna made a coffee cake and everyone rejoiced with the soon-to-be homeowners. Her coffee cake was famous among the neighbors and when the local Catholic parish decided to publish a book of everyone's favorite recipe for a fund raiser, they all wanted her secret recipe for cake. Every cook in the neighborhood bought the book just to get the recipe. But as hard as they tried, no one was successful in baking anything that even closely resembled the cake in taste or appearance. When her daughter questioned her about the ingredients listed in the publication and the complaints that no one could duplicate the cake, she explained, "Lucia, whata you tinga, Betty Crockama givva her besta recipe to alla ofa da peepala?"

While they never knew wealth, she was glad that she was born into the house of Carmine and Lucia Calabrese. She knew the kind of riches that could not be tabulated at a local bank.

Santina walked up the steps and reached for the massive wooden doors of the funeral parlor only to find them locked. She had arrived too early and according to the small sign on the railing, would have to wait almost an hour before the parlor directors would open the doors for viewing. She decided to take a short walk further down Sand Lane in search of a store where she could purchase a box of gum.

As she entered the store, a distinguished man in a dated brown felt fedora called in perfect Italian, "Santina, come stai?" She turned to see a familiar face from her long past.

"Mr. Farina, I'm fine...how are you?" she answered in an excited voice.

"Ima fine, my littla Santina!" he endearingly answered.

Mr. Farina was like a family member ever since he came from Italy in 1913. She remembered accompanying her father to the dock where the boat from Ellis Island emptied its cargo group of immigrants onto Manhattan's shores. Farina was like millions of other southern Europeans who had abandoned their country to come to America. He arrived with his young wife Julietta and their boy Salvatore. He came from *Puglia* and was the son of a family friend who lived there. The two had written letters to each other for a few months before the arrangements could be made for his immigration. A mason by trade, young Ignacio Farina had no trouble finding work in his adopted country and the pieces of his life all seemed to fall into place quickly. But three years after they arrived, his wife died during childbirth. The baby did not survive either.

Santina could still see the immigrant standing over the casket in her parlor. He appeared so much older to her, but in reality, he was only in his mid twenties at the time. Like some people who suffer the loss of a loved one, Farina plunged into his work and became a wealthy man; but he never remarried. She remembered seeing him and his boy, Salvatore, at Mass on Sunday. She grew fond of her adopted cousin, whom she called *Sallyboy*, and would walk to school together. At the local drug store, they spent hours talking about the future and the things they wanted to do when they were older. When she completed eighth grade, Santina left school and went to work at Neuremberg's, while Salvatore went on to study at a trade high school. When he graduated, he became a journeyman welder and took a job building a pipeline in the oil rich southwest. While he promised to write, she received only one post card and then a telegram. He died when a gas line exploded...killing him instantly. In the days that followed, she remembered Mr. Farina coming to her house for dinner. She recalled the silence that filled the dining room as he sat staring at his plate. As a young girl, Santina knew she must be part of that solitude and remained quiet in the house as her father spoke words of consolation. Then one night she heard her father speaking to his forlorn friend in more serious tones.

"No, you dona speak lika this, Ignacio...you go ona...you liva... you dona stoppa! Your wife... she dies, your boy he dies too...but you are here...alive and thissa talk...thissa talk of shooting is wrong. Now givva me the gun!" Then she heard weeping and looked in to see Mr. Farina leaning over the side arm of the couch, sobbing... her father gently patting his back and tearing. It was one of the only times in her life that she witnessed her father crying. He was a strong man...proud and dignified, but not untouched by the pain of others.

One of the troubling questions she asked herself over the years was if her people would have been better off had they stayed in Italy and Sicily. Is a person supposed to leave the land of their birth? She measured the events in this simple man's life and wondered. While he probably would have never have achieved the wealth of this country, might he not have had a better life had he stayed in Puglia? Then she would think of her father and how he came from extreme poverty and settled in America where he found employment and even purchased a house.

Now, she looked across the isle in the drug store to where he was standing. He was no less than two inches shorter then she remembered, but his hair was pure white and full. It's strange, she thought, how in a few seconds she could recall so many events from her past. Here he was...only a few years her senior, but they stood a life-time apart in so many other ways.

"We are all fine, Mr. Farina!" she repeated.

"It'sa so gooda to see you, Santina. Every day, I tink of my paesano, you father, Carmine. If it was notta for him I woulda notta be here. Summaday I go to him and we will play bocce ball and smoka the cigars from our town in Italy - just lika we used to do inna you backayard," the old man said.

Santina walked over and kissed him on the cheek. His unshaved face scraped across her powder make-up, but she didn't mind. He was an old man who found a few moments of happiness in the presence of someone from the past and he needed this...so did she! She watched as he walked out of the store into the open air. He would go to an empty house in South Beach that was filled with rooms of fine imported Italian furniture and the luxuries he had worked so hard for over the years. But she knew he would trade everything he had acquired to live out these golden years sitting next to his childhood sweetheart...Julietta Manganno, the fisherman's daughter from his village! She watched as her father's countryman made his way to the busy street.

Santina paid for her gum and also departed. The sounds that filled the street were different from those she remembered as a child. Back in the old days, Staten Island was a vast open-spaced rural community which lay just across the waters from Manhattan. In the sixties a large bridge was built at the Narrows, joining the small Island with Brooklyn. For Santina, that spelled the end of an era because the Island now teamed with thousands of people filling the streets with noisy cars and buses. The roads were running with impatient and impertinent personalities and she felt that many of the newcomers came to take...not to give. She knew what it was to be a giver...that is the way she was raised. When she was young her father would tell her, *"When Santina Calabrese walka in a rooma she musta bringa the joy and happiness to all offa the people there!"*

Through the years Santina had given so much of her time to others and now she felt tired and weak. Giving will do that!

While the world was changing before her eyes - she clutched the memory of the Island and a time when it was sparsely populated with rural-like hamlets...dotting its quaint and hidden shores.

She opened the small box and a single Chicklet slid down into her hand. She lifted it to her lips that were craving the sweet candy cover, then placed the box in her purse and made her way back to the funeral parlor. Her trek back up the street was tiring. She paused at one point and lifted a paper and pencil from her purse. She scribbled one word, "heart." She would call the doctor on Monday and have her heart checked. She then grumbled to herself and squeezed the note into a ball and threw it in her coat pocket.

"Ah!" she spoke to herself, "I am fine!"

Moments later she walked up the steps of the funeral home, gripped the handrail and half pulled herself to the massive wooden door. She reached for the door handle and completed her short journey through the entrance. Upon entry, she saw the little sign with her friend's name inscribed:

ANGELINA CARUSO
Room B

As she tiptoed through the open door a man dressed in the necessary black suit approached her and spoke in whispers.

"Hello," he said and introduced himself..."I'm the funeral director. We're really not open, but you may sit in the room if you like. I guess I left the door unlocked when I came in a few minutes ago. We don't officially open for another ten minutes!"

Santina nodded her head and whispered, "Thank you, sir."

In the dark of the room, she could see the closed casket covering her friend. In a few moments, someone would come and open it for viewing. Then she would walk to it, kneel and pray... and with her final blessing...the sign of the Cross - she would rise and give the small kneeling bench to the next in line. It was so ritualistic and formal. Unnecessary, she thought. She knew this woman and on any occasion, when they met, they greeted each other with hugs and kisses. Acknowledging her passing could not replace the warmth of her embrace and smile.

Santina questioned the rituals of religion, much the same as her father did. While her mother lived a life of obedience to the church, her father scorned the local priest and all that the Church represented. It was only in his later years that he told Santina about the religion of his ancestors. One day, while walking down a neighborhood street, he related a story to her with a disgust and hatred she had never before seen in him.

At age ten he went with his father to plant trees in the garden between a convent and a monastery. He saw his father lift his shovel revealing a small decaying animal in a clump of mud. The smell filled the little courtyard and he gagged. But it wasn't an animal... it was an unborn baby. His father never spoke about it, but he knew what it was when he heard him curse..."Managgia...the Priest hides this sin in the holy garden!" He threw down his shovel, grabbed his son and hustled him out of the terrace.

Never again was his son required to go to church. Was it an aborted child, fathered by an errant priest? Perhaps it was the grandchild of a dignitary whose daughter had sinned. Was it abortion that was used to cover the transgression? Could this have been the graveyard for bastard children? Many years later...the story still haunted Santina, who wished only to maintain dedicated to her church. Sometimes in the late evening, when she could not find sleep, she would take her Bible and begin to read at random. Her fingers would flick through the pages. She hardly knew of an Old and New Testament and would open to some pages in the middle of the sacred book and began to read. Moments later she would be fast asleep clutching the leather bound volume in her hands.

She knew men and women were fragile...given to selfishness and sin. But she also understood that forgiveness was the only way to live your life in a greedy and selfish world. Despite the confusion about her religion, she knew nothing else and sent her children to Mass every Sunday throughout their childhood. Never did she relate the story to anyone! After all, she thought...God knows!

In the stillness of the room, she sat and could smell the scent of the funeral flowers. Of course they were "funeral flowers," because in any other setting they had a completely different fragrance. To Santina, everything seemed artificial about a funeral home. She studied the various flower arrangements and whispered to the casket.

"Angelina, your family did right by you...your flowers are beautiful! Remember you wanted the clock with the time of your death, you should see the red roses. In case you didn't know, you died at 9:58 am, just before your morning television program. You didn't miss anything. The stories are all the same now, not like in the old days when every week there was a new one. They're not like that anymore, darling. So, now you're in a better place. Give your husband my love. He was a good man...died too soon! You enjoy him now, sweetheart. Me, I'll be with you before you know it. Oh, by the way if you see Francine Giardino tell her that I went to Harry's Department Store in Great Kills and returned the blouse she gave me for a bigger size. I changed the color too, but I don't think she would mind. Tell her, okay!"

"Miss, is everything all right?" The funeral director asked.

"Everything is fine...I'm...I'm...I was just praying," she explained to relieve him from any anxiety he might have about her talking to her old friend.

"Oh....I see!" I'm going to open the doors now...there are people waiting to come in!"

Santina turned to the coffin and spoke. "Angie...your friends have arrived!"

With this, she rose to her feet, walked over to the clothing rack, unbuttoned her coat and lifted it into a wooden hanger. A group of people could be heard out in the foyer and Santina walked just outside of the doors to the room to see who had come. Approaching her was Angelina's daughter, who walked by in a stupor to the casket. She knelt down and began to sob.

"Poor girl," Santina whispered to herself.

She remembered the day her own mother died. She made the funeral arrangements and, like Angelina's daughter, cried and moved in aimless patterns around the room. She remembered the dozen or more guests who filed by her mother's casket. Tear-filled condolences echoed over and over. The room was quiet and reverent until cousin Dominick and his wife Fat Tessie arrived. Cousin Dom walked slowly to the coffin, but Tessie proceeded with less somber movements. Santina had been to enough funerals to know what Fat Tessie was capable of doing when she started her "act."

Sure enough, she broke from her mourning march and ran to the coffin screaming, "LUCIA...LUCIA...MY LUCIA...MY AUNT... MY BEST GIRLFRIEND- COME BAAAACK!" There was a moment of pause...and shock, as everyone in the room looked at the crazy lady who now raised her hands to heaven..."WHY GOD? WHY MY BEST AUNT? MY GIRLFRIEND...WHY?" When her oration was complete, she stepped up on the prayer stool and proceeded to lift her right leg and place it in the casket. "DON'T LEAVE ME...DON'T LEAVE ME, LUCIA...LUCIA!"

When it was obvious she might be successful in joining the dead, the cousins and uncles descended and removed her three hundred sixty-six pound body to the front row of seats! There she sat wailing and talking to herself. Of course, the "bereavement" quickly ended when cousin Dominick announced they were leaving to go to a diner for coffee with some other family members. The antidote for her melodramatic mourning wasn't a sedative...it was the promise of a fresh piece of Italian cannoli pastry! She rose, turned to Santina and in matter of fact tones, said, "Call me...we'll have coffee...I'll bring the pignoli cookies!"

Years later, Santina smiled at the memory of the incident and wondered if anyone would cut loose at Angelina's funeral. While Fat Tessie was gone now for many years, the "torch" had been passed to her daughter, Philomena. Fortunately, while she did know Angelina and would have come to pay her respects, she was on vacation in Florida. The comedy was sure to continue upon her return when she would visit Angelina's daughter…fresh pastries in hand.

Santina watched as several groups of people promenaded into the room. The *Irish side* of Angelina's family arrived and was at the podium signing their names to the registry. Her sister Grace had married a neighborhood boy, Jack Flannery. As it was with many fathers, Angelina's husband, Carmine, usually had a few words of *advice* to give any would-be suitor on the evening of his first date with any of his daughters. He met Jack at the door, stepped outside, closed it behind him and commenced to speak in whispers. While his language was limited, the young suitor would not mistake the words or the intent.

You name issa Jacka, no?...You comma to taka my daughter, Grace, outa, yes?" He asked. Before the lad could reply, the old man leaned forward and whispered.

29

You toucha my daughter witha you stinkin' Irish hands and I blowa your knee-cappasa offa...boom, boom. capisce...you hear?" he spoke using his pointing finger to demonstrate the "boom-boom."

Poor Jack Flanerry nodded his head in complete understanding. The patriarch opened the door and smiled as he led the youth into the living room. All this time, his daughter was listening from the second story window just above the front door. She was mortified... so was Jack! Eleven months later, financially ready and with engagement ring in hand...he asked for her hand in marriage. He thanked the father for his approval and asked if he could now kiss Grace. The father did not answer, but the soon-to-be groom assumed the answer was "no," so he didn't take any chances. Two weeks later, Grace finally leaned over table while eating at a restaurant and kissed him on the lips. Seven years and five children later, it was obvious they had moved beyond the kissing stage. After the fifth child was born, she went for surgery to halt the population explosion. Like many of the other women in the community, Grace Calabrese Flannery had moved from the *edicts* of the church to the *ethics* of society and had her "tubes tied."

Whenever her father met the Family Flannery at the door, he would turn to his wife and announce..."Mrs. Calabrese, you Irisha grandachila are here!" It was no secret...he adored all of his grandchildren...even the Irish ones!

Memories of such things brought a sweet smile to Santina's face. She loved her past...even the hard times...the pain, problems and all that goes with raising a family and interacting with dozens of cousins, aunts, uncles, grandparents and friends. Now she spent her days with visions of the past...when the house was filled with her children scurrying about and playing. She had brought six children into the world and while each had their share of trouble, they grew strong and healthy...marrying and giving Santina and her husband many grandchildren and great-grandchildren. This was the way things were supposed to be for an Italian family...for any family!

Once again she found her way to the same seat she had occupied a few minutes before. As she began to sit down...she noticed a fine mink coat had been draped over the back of the chair next to her.

"Excuse me, is this your seat?" asked a very feminine voice.

"Yes, it is!" answered Santina.

"I'm Susan...Susan Marshall...I'm seeing Marco Caruso."

"I am pleased to meet you, Susan! I'm Santina Fortunato, an old friend of the family," Santina replied, somewhat surprised to see her. Angelina had told Santina all about the *girl* Marco worked with at his company's downtown office.

Susan Marshall had met Angelina's son at work three years before. He was young, she was...older...much older! The two dated for about three months, when Marco announced he was going to bring *the woman from the office*, home for dinner. He told his mother that she was a good girl, worked hard and had never been married. The date was set, the pasta was cooked and the bread was sliced. In the middle of a beautifully set table...mounted a big salad. To the onlooker, one would have gotten the idea she was out to impress her son's date.

It was about five o'clock when the door bell sounded and Angelina went to welcome her boy and his *female guest*. Standing outside of the glass storm door was a beautiful woman, around forty, with long manicured finger nails...a very short skirt and a sweater which did little to conceal that she was indeed a woman. Angelina stood speechless, stammered out a welcome and watched as the storm door was abruptly pushed opened. Her son rushed to her and introduced his date. Then with the enthusiasm of a hungry teenager, he cried, "Mom, I'm starved...where's the macaroni?"

Angelina turned and headed in the direction of the kitchen. At this point, not only was the water for the pasta boiling...but so was the cook. The couple walked into the dining room and sat at the table. A few minutes later, Angelina walked in with a large bowl of spaghetti and meatballs. She moved around the table and began to serve her son. He looked up at her and she looked down. No words were exchanged...there was no need for any. He had seen that look before and knew exactly what his mother was thinking. When she noticed that the girl was staring, she abruptly turned and smiled.

"So, your people are Italian?" she asked as if interrogating a handcuffed prisoner in a police station, knowing exactly what the answer was going to be.

"No, I'm mainly of German descent...with a little of everything else thrown in for good measure. My mother had some American

Indian in her blood too!" she innocently and enthusiastically announced.

"So, you are...Indian?" Angelina continued her interrogation.

"Just a little...way back in my mother's family somewhere," she replied.

"Not Italian...that's too bad," the hostess said sarcastically, then brazenly added, "You are much older than my son!"

A silence now trailed her as she sat down across from the two. Suddenly Angelina cut through the silence...just like the bread knife she was using to dig into the hard-crusted Italian bread before her. She turned to her son with an angry stare and began her planned oration.

"How come you bring this older woman home to me... she is too old for you. She is not even Italian! She looks like a tapinarra!" she angrily called out.

"How come?" he blurted, then continued, "Managgia, mom...I'm a man...I can choose who I want to date!" the son angrily shouted.

Susan lifted the napkin off her knee, placed it on the table, stood and spoke.

"I'm sorry, Mrs. Caruso. I'm sorry that I'm not Italian. I'm sorry that I'm not twenty eight! AND, I'm sorry that I look like a...a... torpedo-nad!"

"We need to leave!" Marco called, as he stood to his feet and moved to take her arm.

"No, Marco...this will never work," Susan started, "I can't change your mother's opinion about me and you can't live with her guilt for the rest of your life. It's better that I leave now...than later," she concluded and made her way to the door. Marco stood to his feet, pushed his chair back to the wall and yelled. "You're not leaving without me, Susan. It's time my mother let go of her little boy and accepted me and whoever I bring into this...this museum!"

The two left through the front door and a dreadful silence filled the room. Angelina sat all alone with a table spread with food and drink. This was the last of her sons...the *unexpected* one...who came late in her life. She had heaped enough guilt on the others and now she was about to lose this one completely. But wasn't this what she was supposed to do? Didn't she know about life and people? Hadn't she lived longer? Didn't she know what was good and bad...right and wrong? Consoled, she wiped her face and cleared the table.

The next day, after work, Marco returned to see her. This time he was alone. He sat his mother down in the dining room and announced he was not going to see Susan again. His mother said nothing, then rose and went into the kitchen. Marco followed close behind and clutched her shoulders as he kissed her on the cheek and spoke, "Mom, I'm a man...I need to make my own decisions. Do you understand?"

Angelina said nothing and continued to stir a large pot of steaming tomato sauce that was bubbling on the stove. Marco left from the back door and locked it behind him. His mother went to her grave thinking her "baby boy" had been saved from worse than death! In spite of Angelina's objection, Marco and Susan dated secretly and now there was more to come.

"Marco and I are going to be married next June," she announced. Santina gazed over at the coffin ...at the *could-have -been mother-in-law*, resting in her coffin.

"That's nice," Santina replied in matter of fact tones.

Susan lifted her coat and spoke, "I'd better be going. I'm meeting a girlfriend for dinner at *Tavern on the Green*. Good bye!"

The Seamstress looked up, smiled and called, "Goodbye!"

Santina watched as the woman moved through the parlor doors and saw her leave from the rear exit to the parking lot. How sad, Santina thought! This was a beautiful and gracious woman who would have made her son proud and been a wonderful daughter-in-law to Angelina. Life is too short...too short for such ignorant anger, she concluded sadly.

Looking up she saw her four girlfriends putting their coats on the clothing rack. Yes, how beautiful they all were, she thought. She remembered the old days when the five of them would walk the streets and hear the whistles and the catcalls from the men passing by.

By her thinking, Carmella was prettiest...with a demure five foot one frame and magnificent legs. In spite of the long dress styles and full blouses, in the old days, one could still see the family genes had not skipped her generation of women. Her older sister Laura was just as beautiful! Carmella never lost her youthful figure. Santina watched as she fitted a full length mink coat into a hanger and the others followed. She studied their faces - then smiled to herself. Yes, her precious girlfriends were feminine and lovely...all dressed up with make-up in the fashion of the models they used to see coming into Neuremberg's shop so many years ago. Time had stood still for them in these matters. It was obvious, like Santina, that the girls also coveted those days of glamour and grace - even if they looked totally out of place with the newer styles.

"Tina! Tina," cried Carmella using a favorite nickname for her friend.

"Carmella, how are you, my darling sister?" Santina replied watching her girlfriend make their way through the isle and chairs to reach her. They all embraced and kissed. This was their custom... one of love adoration and respect. Santina was the oldest...and in respect for "their elder," the girls always yielded the head chair at a restaurant or front seat in a cab to her. This was the kind of esteem for maturity that shaped their culture and friendship.

However, one day Santina complained about the treatment.

"I feel like your mother when you treat me like this!" I'm two years older than the oldest of you and you make me feel like it is twenty-two years!"

"Someone has to be the mamma when we get together...so you are the MAMMA!" Carmella laughingly explained.

From that day on, Santina smiled and accepted her honored position. She loved the girls as if they were blood and there was no higher praise then to be considered *blood* of another Italian family. Her role, however, was somewhat usurped about a year after they started working for the Brothers Neuremberg.

It was Josephina who discovered that Isadore was peering into the dressing room through a tiny hole above the mirror. He watched each morning when the five would strip down to their slip. He must have done this from their first day on, but it was Josephina who figured it out when she heard someone fall in the adjourning room. She told the girls about it and Santina was incensed. That was the day they decided the 'oldest' should handle the problem. She told the girls that she would meet and confront the peeping tom.

"NO, I'll handle this my own way!" Josephina protested.

"You cannot accuse this man of this because you don't know for sure if he is really peeking," Santina offered.

"NONSENSE! He's peeking all right and if you go to him, you'll get fired. Let me handle him!" Over the objections of the "eldest," Josephina made it a point to be last to leave the store one night. The girls were to wait downstairs at Duffy's.

When the workday was officially over, Santina, Carmella, Adelina and Lucia hurried to the dressing room, changed and made a fast exit to the street. Josephina continued to work on one last piece before she yawned, stretched and looked around the now empty workroom. When she noticed Isadore standing in front of the office door, she sauntered seductively over to the little changing room. Then she took a few steps, paused and bent down to fix her stocking. The *seductress* raised her dress above her knee and looked at Isadore, who was now staring at her with piercing eyes. He moved quickly into the adjacent small storage closet as Josephina took her time before reaching the door to the changing room. She positioned herself so Isadore could see her every move, then paused to hear the stillness of the shop. No one was moving now. She imagined that Isadore's eye was glued to the little opening and moved ever so slowly to the side where she was out of his view. She began to sing out loud and readied for the "attack."

She reached into her purse and took out an ink pen that had been filled an hour before when the plan was concocted. She slowly moved the pen upward against the wall and stopped a few inches before reaching the carefully chiseled aperture. She held her breath and moved the pen closer to the hole, slipping her long fingernail into the gold ink release lever as she did. Now she moved the pen tip closer to the target area. She checked to see that her long fingernail was securely under the release mechanism, took a breath and lifted it quickly. Blue ink squirted out and began to flow down the wall in front of her, but wasn't certain if it had reached Isadore's eager eye. She raised her voice and sang louder, moving quickly to remove her smock and place her street clothing over her trembling body.

In a few seconds Josephina emerged from the sanctuary, which of late, had been infiltrated by the lustful eyes of her employer. A moment later she appeared down on the street and rushed into the candy store. There she found the girls giggling as she made her entrance and then proceeded to replay the whole affair for their eager ears.

They left the candy store and headed for the subway. It was Friday and they would not be able to certify whether the *mission* had been successful until Monday morning. They held their breath in anxious anticipation.

On Monday morning they stood outside the shop waiting for Isadore. Sure enough, he came down the street in his usual stride, but there was something different about his appearance. He was fully dressed in a long coat...capped by a fedora and a hanging scarf that was draped over his face in such a way as to reveal only his eyes. Of course such attire would be quite acceptable considering the cold winter months in New York City; but there was a slight problem in justifying his winter garb. It was April!

"All right...all right...let's get started," he bellowed.

When the girls finally reached their machines and started sewing, Isadore rushed by them in a phobic frenzy with a bolt of fabric hiding his face. Ever clumsy, he tripped on a loose floor board and went stumbling across the room. The bolt of fabric flew into the air, finally coming to rest on Aldo's work table. When Isadore stopped rolling, he lay flat on his back with the five girls hovering over him...staring in amazement at his face...his navy blue face.

The employees stood speechless as they gazed at Josephina's artwork. It was all too perfect! Lying in front of them, after a humiliating fall, was their Peeping Tom. From his brow to just below his nose, was a perfect outline of the *Lone Ranger's* mask, perfectly tattooed by a chance squirting of indelible pen ink.

A few days later the dressing room had a fresh coat of paint and the hole was sealed! The girls made a daily inspection of Josephina's artwork and watched as the weeks rolled by and the "mask" begin to dissipate into Isadore's natural flesh tones. To the average on-looker the coloration was gone, but the girls swore that three months later they could still see the borders of the mask. So much for voyeurs in the garment district!

Brother Harry was something else! He had an eye for the ladies and exercised his wishful thinking in the matter of one of his biggest customers, Hazel Roth. There was a mutual attraction and such is to be respected in the relationship of a man and a woman, but there was one catch. Harry was married! No, he was very married...with three children, a mortgage and the understanding that if he didn't work...he didn't eat. But that was all made to be a little more complicated because his father-in-law bailed out the business when the brothers lost their lease and were left with no option but to purchase the building. His wife Edna was a domineering witch who held the whole matter over his head with a deed that would revert to her if there ever were any "improprieties."

So why does a man seek another relationship when there is so much at stake?

"Are you crazy? That buttinski you married will bury us! We'll be left with nothing but two bobbins, a boutonniere and an empty bottle of borscht!" shouted brother Isadore when he found out about the relationship.

"It's love!" answered Harry.

"LOVE? LOVE? I'LL GIVE YOU LOVE...MY TUCHAS IT'S LOVE!" bellowed his brother, raising his hands to his head in disbelief.

Harry might have gone unnoticed by his wife, but nothing good lasts forever. For that matter, nothing bad hangs around for long either. It happened one Saturday morning when Harry told his wife he had to go to the store and work on some papers. He had other things to work on as well. Who said the wife is the last to know? Edna followed her scoundrel husband and found him in the arms of another woman atop a mound of soft imported designer fabric on Aldo's work table.

On Monday morning Harry showed up with a broken nose, black eye and a torn ear lobe. Hazel was never seen in the shop again, but Antoinette thought she saw a woman who looked like her on the street a few days later, except she was wearing a wig and heavy make-up. When Josephina found clumps of red hair mingled in some sample swatches under Aldo's table, the girls began to sum what happened. Edna beat them both up and literally kicked the home wrecker down the stairs and into the streets. As for Harry, his temptations waned when reality set in and from that day forward, he was ever faithful...but he hated Edna nonetheless.

Santina was not the only one who had to confront the brothers on "issues" of concern. When Carmella showed up for her first day of work it was Isadore who *toured* her around the facility. She was only sixteen and he must have been out of his mind to think he stood a chance at wooing her into any relationship or liaison. But try he did for the first few weeks. She would receive flowers from a *secret admirer* or candy from an *interested party*. Josephina had no trouble uncovering the suitor because the flowers were the cheapest bundle the local florist would deliver and the candy usually came from his house. In spite of it all, Carmella was excited that a man found her attractive and was paying attention to her. But no matter how hard the girls tried to convince her, she could not believe that her suitor was Isadore. Finally, Josephina set out to unmask him and prove it to her. What she didn't reason were the consequences for all of the girls if her boss ever found out about her scheme. But youth does not pretend to find logic in mischief.

She decided to set a trap and once and for all convince Carmella that her secret admirer was none other than her ugly boss. She asked Antoinette to arrange for her brother Vinny to be at Luna's Restaurant on Mulberry Street at six o'clock on a Friday night. She then sent a message to Isadore that the "object of his affection" would like to meet him for dinner. To set the stage, she convinced Carmella that she had been wrong and that her suitor was not Isadore after all, but a nice man who had come into the shop and noticed her.

On Friday, Carmella brought a change of clothes and all day dreamed about her "date." Vinny confirmed that he would be there waiting for her. Up until now he had never met the little seamstress, but didn't need a detailed description to isolate a teenage female in a restaurant. The girls chuckled as they watched Isadore coming down the street that morning carrying a change of clothing under his arm. They laughed, as twice he dropped his package on the concrete and fell one time himself when he bent down to pick it up. He too was ready to suit up for the evening. They spent an uneventful day at the shop and chewed their perfectly manicured nails in anticipation of the evening's events.

At six o'clock Vinny was already sitting in a booth at the restaurant with his eyes fixed on the front door. Josephina and the girls banked on Isadore being late, but took no chances. During the day one of his dress shoes was lifted and placed far under one of the desks in his office. Little Carmella left work a little after five, all dressed up, and headed for Mulberry Street with Adeline. She arrived at Café Luna right on time and scanned the restaurant as she crossed the front door. Vinny rose to his feet, smiled and waved. Her little heart leaped as the tall, dark and handsome boy rose to his feet. A late teen himself, Vinny was the pride of the family...the first to go to college.

Carmella walked lightly to the booth and her Italian Prince Charming asked for her coat. It was her very first date. Her father and mother had granted permission because one of the girls was supposed to accompany her. Indeed one did, because Adeline fixed herself just outside of the eatery and looked through the window and kept a watchful eye on the booth.

At six twenty, late as predicted, a gaunt figure...with a familiar awkward gait came running down the busy street. It was Isadore. Adeline intercepted him as he ran to the door.

"Mr. Neuremberg, Mr. Neuremberg," she stammered out as if out of breath then continued...her words racing. "It's a good thing I got here in time. We all figured that you were the one who was sweet on Carmella and we found out that her father and uncle don't want any man to get near her. In fact, they know about her date tonight and they're on their way over now to shoot the guy who is supposed to meet her."

"Oh, no! I gotta get out of here before they come...thank you, thank you for warning me...Oh, my...I don't know what to do?"

"Well, they'll be here any moment and you don't have a moment to lose," she instructed him.

The secret admirer stood frozen in his tracks and continued to stutter out his appreciation, when Adeline turned him around and pointed him in the direction from which he had come. He literally scooted down the street like a three year old and kept calling out, "She saved my life...she saved my life...she saved my life!" A few moments later the wishful suitor disappeared around the corner.

Adeline looked in the window to see two smiling teens peering over a menu...and each other. Vinny was beaming and Carmella never looked prettier.

A year and eight months later they were married.

End of story? Not quite? On Monday Isadore didn't show up for work. According to his brother Harry, he was "out of town." To bring an end to the terror, Santina announced to the girls, loud enough so that everyone in the shop could hear, that Carmella's father and uncle found some guy hanging around Carmella and he was now walking with a limp. Standing within hearing distance was Harry who had arrived early that day to open the store. He turned and ran into his office, closed the door and called his brother to tell him the coast was clear. Convenient for the girls was that small closet next to the brothers' office where they could monitor all conversations... when necessary. Fifty years later they were still laughing about the incident.

End of story? Not yet! One day when Isadore overheard the girls bragging about their exploit, he called the ringleader into his office and threatened to fire her. But she had a *trump card*!

Josephina had never told the girls that she witnessed him frequenting the well known Madame Lee's underground brothel in China Town or that on a certain Friday in June, in the late afternoon, a special visitor came to his office. Somehow she knew the information would come in handy and when he called her into his office, she smiled inside and knew it was time to blow the whistle! And she did!

"So you're a big shot...getting involved with my affairs," Isadore protested.

"Now, Izzy...I can call you that, can't I? I'm sure the girls at Madame Lee's call you...Izzy, don't they?" Josephina whispered in soft mesmeric tones.

"What I do is my business and not yours!" her boss informed her.

"When it comes to Carmella, it is my business! She's my...my cousin!" Josephina sarcastically lied.

"Oh, I didn't know that!" he replied.

"So, let's just call it even... I keep my job and I respectfully call you, Mr. Neuremberg again...just like old times," she grinned and spoke as she turned and walked out of the room, allowing her long, red painted nails to trail around the door jam as she did.

From that point on the incident was not reviewed and never again did Isadore attempt to date any of the girls.

End of story? Well, almost! Vinny and Carmella had four boys and two girls!

The years that passed at the shop were not without adventure for the five little Italian princesses. Each grew to become more and more independent and wise to the ways of the world. They knew only the innocence of a guarded youth and their morals transcended the little temptations that confronted them. But the "shenanigans" of the Neuremberg's never seemed to end.

One day Harry called Antoinette into his office and closed the door.

"Antoinette, I need you to do something for the company," he began. The young seamstress dreamed of modeling some of the clothing the company offered and wondered if her big chance had come.

"Now I know you've been interested in modeling some of our clothes for the clients when they inspect our goods each August and I think we can use your talents. There is one thing I need you to do for us," he began.

"Oh, Mr. Neuremberg, anything to help the company," she enthusiastically interrupted.

"That's good! Now here is what we need. You and I know that we buy from several jobbers and our material is of excellent quality. My brother and I have decided to branch out a bit and sell some pre-manufactured clothing. What we need for you to do is stay late this Friday night and cut the other manufacturer's label out and sew ours in its place."

Innocently, Antoinette looked up at her boss and spoke.

"But Mr. Neuremberg, that's not right. If we didn't make the dress, how can we put our label in it? Oh, I couldn't do that!" she insisted.

"Listen, this is your opportunity to help the company and if you help the company, we'll help you! You'll make a wonderful model for us and we can get you away from the humiliating work you do upstairs," he tempted her.

"I don't think it's humiliating, Mr. Neuremberg!" she answered.

"What do you want to do... sew pieces of cloth for the rest of your life?" he fired back in anger.

"Mr. Neuremberg, if I sew your label into the clothing, it would be like lying and if I lie for you...aren't you afraid...I will lie to you some day?"

"Well...you know, sometimes you have to fudge a little bit in business," he retorted in a huff.

Silence filled the room and little Antoinette turned and walked out. Nothing more was ever said about the issue and he never challenged the character of the five girls again.

It was Aldo Manucci who came to understand the real character of the *Neuremberg Twins,* as he would call them. Like most "foreigners," he came to America with a dream and when he arrived at their shop...he woke up.

Arthur Neuremberg and his brother Julius founded the business on two principles: *take the customers for all they were worth and give them a product that was just good enough so they wouldn't and couldn't bring it back.*

Of course, they never actually used those words, but the daily operation of the company revealed their unwritten *business code.*

It was the "good enough product" that Aldo had to deal with when he forged a new pattern or wanted a cloth that was more expensive then the stock materials. The *entrepreneurs* bought the cheapest material and demanded no scraps be thrown away after a cutting. In spite of their frugality, Aldo did produce a beautiful garment for them.

"Iffa you put thissa cloth for the coata, the people will buy it because it wear better and lasta longer," Aldo proclaimed one day when he sat with the brothers in their office trying to convince them to purchase better material. Actually, he wasn't sitting...they were... on plush leather chairs.

"We'll look into it," replied Arthur. They looked into it all right; and when they found out how much it would cost....looked the other way. Aldo knew never to go back into the office and challenge them. Oh, there was one other time when he absolutely would not tolerate their dealings.

It was a few months after he was hired as a part time employee, that he was summoned into the office.

"Aldo...how are you making out here in America?" he asked.

"Good...thissa country issa good!" He replied.

"You know, I spoke to Julius and he says you can really cut a piece of cloth!" What he failed to say was that Aldo Manucci was the best designer and cutter they ever had working for them.

"Graze...I say...ah, tanka you, Mr. Neurembergama," he answered respectively.

"You know, we might need another presser real soon and if you are interested in steady work, you could cut part time and press part time. Then you could work full time for us," came the offer.

"This issa gooda...I needa the money to bringa mamma anda my sisita froma the old country. How mucha you pay for thissa work?" Aldo questioned.

"Well, let's see! We pay you five dollars a week for cutting and we...we can pay you another four dollars for pressing. How does that sound?" The store owner offered.

"But you pay, Mr. Figgalicci tenna dollars for fulla time. Iffa I worka haffa time, how comma I dona getta haffa the money he getta," he innocently and correctly questioned.

"These foreigners, telling me what to pay them," his boss mumbled resentfully under his breath.

"Mr. Neurembergama, you aska me if I want to work fulla time. Si...ah, yes. I need to worka fulla time; but I needa fulla pay," Aldo responded.

"Okay, I'll tell you what...you press for a few weeks and we'll see if we can...if we can pay you half of what we pay Gennaro Figgalicci," came the counter offer from the senior Neuremberg.

"Mr. Neurembergama...halfa time and halfa pay equalla to fulla time," was the confident reply from the immigrant.

"Okay...okay!" the shop owner indignantly replied.

For several weeks Aldo designed, cut and pressed. Finally, the chief pattern maker left when he got an offer from Shapiro's down the street. When Julius finished cursing his competition, Aldo was offered the position.

In the garment industry, staying ahead of the competition was the most important thing in maintaining business. When a style changed it meant a costly investment in what was known as standard trade patterns. These patterns were expensive and sometimes were replaced by newer styles within weeks. Obviously, the brothers were always looking for ways of cutting costs on anything that might result in more profit. By now they knew that they should never confront the girls with anything which might compromise their values. But one day after they received a report on sales, Arthur brought in a dress and asked Aldo to do something that might be considered illegal. The way the brothers figured it...such a practice would only be *illegal* if they got caught!

"Aldo, disassemble this dress...you know what I mean...take it apart, copy the design, sew it up again and bring it back to Guttenberg's and get a refund," the proprietor spoke in matter of fact words.

Knowing exactly what they were suggesting, little Aldo acted out his words with just the right amount of ignorance and insight to convince them he didn't quite understand their request.   "What is it thatta you want to, Mr. Neurembergama?"

"Copy this dress...Oh, you know what I mean!" his boss reiterated, now in insistent anger.

"Mr. Neurembergama, this dressa was mada fromma a man... from his owna mind. He no copy fromma somebody. Iffa you wanna new style, I givva you one. I no needa to copy," Aldo replied.

"I want it copied!" came the stern and demanding reply.

The room grew quite as Aldo walked over to his little locker, lifted his lunch box and placed it on a cutting table. Expressionless, he pushed his work to the side. Still wordless, he began to unbutton his smock. It was obvious he would rather walk out than do what he was asked to do. Panic filled the air! Arthur began to bumble out his pleadings. Losing this craftsman might set the brothers back for weeks...maybe months as they would have to steal a designer from the competition. The anxious reaction was predictable.

"No, no...don't take your smock off...ah, forget the whole matter," the nervous boss bellowed.

"Mr. Neurembergama, I comma to thissa country to givva...notta to steala fromma nobody," Aldo courageously spoke.

Listening to the entire conversation was Antoinette. She smiled at the courage of her countryman and never forgot the honesty and innocence with which he handled their boss. She told the girls about the incident and one of the older Chinese women who worked part-time in the packing department sang out, "She likee Aldo, she likee Aldo!"

During those first few months when Aldo began working at the shop, it was Antoinette who conveniently always had an extra sandwich and a thermos full of fresh coffee to share. If the way to a man's heart was through his stomach, Antoinette was not taking any chances.

She liked him and she decided he would be a wonderful husband for her children...the seven she intended on having. Six months later they were married. They had their differences, but then doesn't everyone? When one considers the differences two individuals bring to a union, there is nothing that a little hard work and understanding cannot remedy. The seamstress sized up her man and knew exactly what needed to be changed. But there was one feature which she would have difficulty altering, unless she had a secret formula! Antoinette stood five four and Aldo was just a coat button above five feet. But...it was a match.

Aldo was a gentle man, talented and determined to make it America. In Italy, his family members were farmers and he might have followed in their line of work and headed for the fields at the ripe old age of eight; but one day, when they inventoried the demure youngster, they found that he could not touch the ground with his fingers. His Uncle Franco announced that Aldo would go to trade school and become a tailor. So much for short arms! Twenty three years later, he was living in America on the lower eastside on Broome Street...a quiet bachelor and tailor. And he still couldn't touch the ground!

Aldo never asked Antoinette to marry him...it was his mother. When he was finally able to afford passage for her, the matriarch came to America holding two old valises fastened with twine and his younger sister, Maria, standing at her side.

One Sunday, Antoinette and her sister Rose Angela dropped off Aldo's paycheck and his mother invited the girls in for coffee. No matter how poor, hospitality among the Italians was part of the culture and of course, the girls accepted the invitation. Before eating, Aldo, a good Catholic son, lowered his head and offered the blessing for the refreshments. Aldo's head was bowed, Maria's head was bowed, Antoinette's head was bowed and Rose Angela's head was bowed. But not Aldo's mother! She had one eye on Aldo, one on Antoinette and one looking heavenward. She quickly sized up the situation.

"You are married, si?" she questioned Antoinette as she smiled and filled her cup with steaming espresso coffee.

"No, Mrs. Manucci, I'm the old maid in my family. I won't get married until I find a good man," she replied as Aldo's mother passed a tray of fig cookies...with a big smile on her face.

She knew a good man. In fact, she knew a perfect man and happened to know him personally. He was sitting at the table across from her.

"Aldo is not with a wife yet, but we look for a good girl for him," she announced.

"You live with your people?" came the next inquiry from Aldo's benefactor.

"Oh, yes...I wouldn't think of leaving home like the American girls do until I get married," Antoinette replied.

"Thatsa good...you are a gooda girl," the matchmaker-mother agreed, adding, "Not lika the Americana girls."

When the girls left the table and walked into the parlor, Aldo grumbled.

"Mamma, why do you aska thissa girl about marriage?" he asked anxiously.

"Shut up and go into the parlor...don't ask you mother why she says something," came the reply. You might expect that if his father was living, it might have gone a little differently. In Aldo's home his father reigned. Well at least that's what everyone thought when they looked in on the family. Yes, he did reign, but mamma usually called the shots in a good portion of the issues confronting the daily life of the family. In this case, Aldo's mother would have listened to her husband respectfully...then told them BOTH to go to the parlor.

The next Tuesday night came and Aldo and Antoinette sat across the table from their parents. The melodic tones of their Italian language filled the air. There was laughter and deep conversation... questions and answers. The next time the families met they were at a Chinese Restaurant. The large neon light blazing the words, *China Town Chow Mien,* could be seen reflecting off the black suit of the groom through the second floor window of the restaurant. He looked up and danced the first dance with his new bride. If Italians went out to eat...it was usually at a Chinese Restaurant. Many a wedding was celebrated over chop suey and fried rice. It was a festive occasion with all the family present. Adeline's two aged uncles, Benito and Guido, were there and like several others, brought two large loaves of Italian bread and a bottle of homemade wine.

The funeral parlor now began to bustle with conversations here and there. She looked over at Antoinette and just like Aldo's mother, she was strong and feisty. Who says a man doesn't marry someone like his mother?

Several months after the wedding, two important events transpired: Antoinette was pregnant with their first child and the Neuremberg brothers retired transferring the partnership to Arthur's sons. She worked throughout her pregnancy.

Santina looked up and saw Josephina inching her way through the isle to greet her. She was a sweet girl who went through life as a giving and loving soul. Life had been difficult. She lost her husband when he was thirty seven. Santina always hoped that she would remarry, but now all these years later she was single.

Perhaps the word *single* was inappropriate, thought Santina. "Single" meant she had never married and had no partner or mate. There was not a day that went by that Josephina did not speak of her husband and their love...if not by words, then the gaze in her eyes when she saw the other girls with their husbands.

During those years, just after her husband died, she found comfort in her two boys...Ralph and Vincent. They both finished high school and immediately signed up for active duty on the high seas.

Josephina had saved money and would await their return so she could send them both to some college. She hoped they might become doctors or teachers. After her husband's death, she relocated to the south shore of Staten Island in the little hamlet of Great Kills. There she raised her family.

But in June of 1944 two young and distinguished soldiers appeared at her door carrying a black leather case. She looked into their eyes and watched as they saluted her. How strange she thought. Why were they saluting her? Then one lifted a black attaché case, opened it in one abrupt ritualistic movement and handed her a letter from the Department of the Navy. She looked down at the gloved hand of the soldier and took it gently from him.

She paused and looked into their young, ruddy faces, then began to open the seal. She had not heard from the boys in weeks and seconds of hope and fear passed until she finally could focus on the text.

"Here, you read it for me," she whispered and handed it to one of the soldiers.

"But....we're not...., he replied as he held the letter.

"Please," Josephina interrupted. The soldier poised himself in an attempt to look and sound official and then read it to her.

"We regret to inform you that your sons, Ralph and Vincent Mura were killed this morning in battle. They served their country with..."

"No, don't finish...don't speak...I know how they served, they are my sons," she said, with head bowed.

To keep her mind busy, she went back to work for a time at Neuremberg's, but within a few months realized she could no longer deal with the hours of travel and found employment at Larsen's Department store in Great Kills, a few blocks from her house.

"Josie," Santina affectionately called as they neared to embrace.

"Can you believe Angelina is gone?" Josephina asked.

"Sweet Angelina," Santina replied.

"Yes, Sweet Angelina," Josephina confirmed.

"And how are you, Josie?" Santina asked.

"I'm all right!" she replied.

Santina could not reckon the loneliness of a woman in a house... all alone for so many years. Her family was her life...with all of the happiness and heartache. She could only imagine the stillness of her day. There would be few phone calls or visits...but hardest of all to imagine, there were no memories of a father and sons and all that they might have done together.

Josie would pass through this world with no remnant of her family. Yes, her two sisters had large families, but one lived in California and the other in Italy. There would be no passion for the future...only the companionship of late night television movies. First, she would listen to the news at six o'clock, eat a quiet dinner then retreat to a small bedroom and single bed. There she would stare at the television until programming ceased in the wee hours of the morning.

Even though Santina had lost her husband years before, the full bed held his place and she would sometimes turn and call his name... not realizing from her deep sleep that he was no longer there. Like Josie, when the morning skies filled with light, she would go to her kitchen and bake or clean or do something a homemaker does to redeem the silence of the earth at that time. But the solitude would be broken when someone called or came by for an unexpected visit.

On one occasion Josephina, confided that she longed for the touch of a man...that inexplicable and intimate feeling that men and women share...even when they don't touch. She met a man one night at a wedding reception and struck up a conversation. Two days later, as she was about to invest her emotions in him, she felt the groove of a wedding ring on his left hand. She confronted him, he confessed and that was the end of it. Josephina had become vulnerable and she almost yielded her emotions and morals to a stranger. Her loneliness was like a quiet companion - speechless and relentless.

There was another occasion when Josephina was again confronted with the unruly passions of others...the kind that destroys the very soul of a woman and good marriages. It was on a trip to see her two sons at Fort Dix, just before they were to leave for active duty. The military-sponsored bus ride from Grand Central Station to Fort Dix found her among other parents of enlisted men.

When she boarded, little did she know that her two day visit would bring her face to face with a horrible experience...one that would secure her morals...forever. No thought of unfaithfulness, even to a man who had died years before, ever bridged her mind because she lived in a time when brides echoed, "I do" and meant it. It was a time when nothing could compromise the sanctity of a marriage...in life or death.

The scandals of Hollywood and Broadway stars ended an *age of virtue* that had dominated mid twentieth century Catholic women. The titillation of stories in the local news and ladies magazines somehow made the idea of sex an option to those who found themselves in those moments when only passion dominated the psyche.

Her visit to see her sons was a last minute decision as the boys were ready to ship out in a few days. Perhaps she wouldn't see the boys for six months or a year. Her trip to Fort Dix was uneventful.

Josephina checked into a local motel with some of the other parents. Over a Navy sponsored dinner, she met Gary and Anne McNally, the parents of another boy about to leave for overseas duty. Anne was a gracious mid-westerner, who had a bouffant hairstyle and spoke with a spoiled innocence. Surely she was a woman of wealth and privilege with the luxury of a maid and gardener. Her husband Gary was a cordial gentleman who also reflected wealth. Perhaps he owned a company or was an executive in a firm. She concluded they were upper middle class. By their standards Josephina was a poor working woman, the kind who lived on a fixed income and rigid budget - purchasing only that which was needed. Her clothing also indicated her economy.

On the evening of the first night pleasant conversation filled the banquet room. It was Gary who suggested they go elsewhere to finish out the day. Without caution, Josephina took what would turn out to be a foolish liberation from her conservative ways and followed them out of the door. Gary hailed a cab and a moment later the car moved into the thoroughfare.

"Take us to George's Pub," he ordered the driver with a familiarity that concerned the innocent seamstress.

The confidence with which he spoke, and the awareness of the strange pub, brought a cautious fear over Josephina. What was she doing in this cab...with these unfamiliar people, in a strange place. Now she could only wish the night away.

The cab pulled up to a small restaurant stationed just off the busy highway. It was dark and dreary and Josephina's fear was evident by the far away look Gary gave her and the words he spoke.

"Hey, Josie...relax! A few drinks and you'll be fine!"   T h e words were far less then what she needed to sedate her emotions, but when his hand reached for hers, she began to calm. She repented to herself for the spent anxious emotions and followed the couple out of the car. She must put aside childish restraints and give herself the luxury of a "free evening." It was a grown up thing to do...and it was time for her to grow up, she thought.

They walked to the entrance where an unfriendly smoke-filled atmosphere jumped into her innocent face. The fleeting seconds of her introduction to the seedy, dark and dismal bar atmosphere told her she was far removed from the clean air in the parlor of her own house. Each morning, rain or shine, she would raise her windows to allow the cool morning Staten Island breezes to filter through her rooms. Now there was a scent of dirt in the air.

Of all the girls, Josie was the tidiest homemaker...always cleaning and arranging. They would tease her that when she got to heaven...she would find something to clean.

Gary clutched her arm and that of his wife and strolled into the dimly lit bar area. The darkness confirmed she didn't belong in the setting. The three moved quickly to a booth and before he even sat down, Gary ordered a scotch and soda then turned to his wife, who mouthed, "*Honey...the usual!*" Josephina sat stunned, not knowing what to say, let alone give an order for a drink. She stumbled through her words and finally requested a glass of ginger ale.

"Ginger ale?" Gary bellowed.

"I'm not a drinker," Santina sheepishly and almost apologetically replied, as if she had to say something as to not offend the couple. Then something strange happened. A man, who seemed to come from nowhere, moved to the booth and sat down next to her.

"This is my brother Carl," the wife introduced, rising to peck him on the cheek.

"How nice, I, I...I'm pleased to meet you!" Josephina again, stumbling with her words.

The next hour and half went by with small talk and drinking. Carl was single...at least that is what he professed.

"Hey, let's all dance," he suggested.

"I don't know if I...." came Josephina's reply.

"Ah come on...you two look like a great couple together," Gary demanded as he pushed Josephina from the seat into the waiting arms of his brother-in-law.

She went cold...almost frozen as she unwillingly yielded to the stranger's arms and hands. On the dance floor the innocent touching of a man and woman should have ignited unavoidable passions, but she loathed the moments of this specious union.

The evening moved as predicted...moment by moment, with no respect for Josephina's wishes that it would end quickly...even abruptly.

The minutes turned to nearly three hours and finally a cab brought all four back to the banquet hall, which was a few blocks from the motel area. Understanding her vulnerability in a strange city, she accepted Carl's offer to walk her to the hotel. The couples separated and she began to walk slowly. Next to her was a stranger...someone she knew nothing about. As they crossed the intersection and eyed the hotel's lights, Santina felt elated that she would be in her temporary home in a few moments. It was not her real home, but the borrowed accommodation hundreds must have stayed in before...the space she had conscientiously dusted and scrubbed earlier.

Their steps were slow and a few times they paused to comment on something they were discussing. Finally, within eye-shot of the motel, Carl seemed to scoop her in his arms and kiss her. Santina's mind raced with thoughts of rape and injury.

"No," she screamed.

"NO?" he echoed in a kind of disbelief.

"No, let me alone, or I'll scream for help," she now demanded.

"Hey, don't play that married stuff with me. Your old man is dead and as for me, well, when a man is hundred miles from home, he is no longer married...that's the way I see it," he replied.

"A hundred miles...a thousand miles, I am married and you cannot have me...now or ever," she cried out angrily in reply.

"Okay, lady...but you could have had a good time," he now said in drunken tones.

"You are drunk...and I don't like you! You go now and leave me alone," she ordered.

For Josephina there was no compromise in her marriage. Arturo would have her full devotion and love forever...even in death. Oh, there were times when well-meaning friends introduced her to eligible bachelors and widowers, but no one would replace her one and only groom.

As for Arturo, however, there was one indiscretion for which he was forever repentant. It was several years after they were married, that he came home late...very late one Friday night. He entered their apartment quickly, mumbled how dirty he was then shed his clothing and ran to the bathroom. He locked the door and showered. Twenty minutes later he emerged smiling and babbling about his day at work. Josephina moved to kiss him on the cheek, but he grabbed her and kissed her passionately. His shower and cologne drenched face had successfully masked the perfume she would smell on his shirt the next day as she placed it into the washing machine.

During the next few weeks, twice she would raise the phone to be greeted by a hang-up after she answered, "Hello."

If the warning, *you can be sure your sins will find you out,* held true, then eventually her husband would be caught in his sin.

But it was a few weeks later when Josephina was on the front porch as Arturo arrived home much later then usual. The unmistakable scent of *Evening in Paris*, mingled with his own perspiration could not camouflage the fact that he indeed had been in the presence of a woman...close presence!

She stood and raised her head to meet his eyes. Then she embraced and kissed him...while whispering in his ear.

"How was your *Evening...Evening in Paris*, my husband?

The guilty froze in his embrace and clutched his wife...holding her for what seemed like minutes. He freed her then went into the foyer and on up the stairs to their bathroom. There he attempted to wash his guilt away with soap and water in an endless shower.

They never spoke of the events of that evening again. And never again did Arturo come home late or did his body have any foreign odor...the kind that clings to a man's skin and tells a story. He went to his grave thinking that Josephina would never learn about the Irish woman at work that he once referred to as "the pretty cleaning lady." She did see her one time when she picked Arturo up at work. The woman was taller and stood on spindly legs. For a moment Josephina hated and despised this strange woman. A fleeting moment of hurt and anxiety gripped and held her captive to ideas of confrontation and revenge. But the flirtation had been several years before and she would not allow herself the passion of these emotions. Hatred for another human was an investment she could and would not make.

The faithful wife never forgot the Sunday morning after she had confronted her husband on the porch. She saw him go forward in church to receive communion and watched as he pushed the hand of the priest, refusing to accept the round wafer. He returned to his seat and stared ahead. Tears squeezed through his eyes and he held back his repentant emotions. Josephina reached across to his knee and patted him.

In a quiet moment that same week, Josephina thought about Arturo. Most men would ultimately confess to their adultery out of guilt. But confession did not necessarily guarantee repentance. Josephina reasoned that Arturo's confession to God was sincere and remorseful. If God could forgive her husband, she must also do the same. She never allowed her hurt to change her love for this man and did nothing to show the pain she felt inside...and there was pain.

In the early days, while working at the store, she did fantasize about marriage and a certain Prince Charming.

The shop, with all of its mundane tasks, provided opportunities for the girls to reach beyond their little world and meet the exceptional and the elite. Buyers traveled to the garment district from all over the world.

Of all the customers who came into the little run-down clothier shop, no one impressed the girls more than Ettore Bertolucci. He was tall and graceful…the kind of man that dominates his sex and exuded wealth and station. He stood six feet two inches, plus two and half more inches provided by his designer shoes. The high heeled footwear and his graceful, almost feminine manner brought suspicion that Ettore was the "other kind" of man…a finocchio!

"Isn't he beautiful," Josephina sang out the first time she saw the dark stranger coming into the shop

The girls all looked in amazement at the impeccable specimen standing before them.

"This is Count Ettore Bertolucci," announced Julius.

The girls stood silent and amused at their boss's reverence for a potential customer. Somehow, the elder Neuremberg knew how to put on the airs…even disguising his ancestry with perfect diction and a complete eraser of his over-pronunciation "big words"…the kind he loved to use to impress his customers." But the verbal masquerade only lasted for a few sentences. Then his over-pronunciation of the final consonant would ultimately betray him. He couldn't escape his dramatic over-use of word endings like, whattt and thattt.

His introduction, which provided a first and last name, preceded by his title, assured the girls that they were to respectfully acknowledge their guest.

"Speaking for the girls," Josephina called out confidently. "We are all pleased to meet you Mr. Bertolucci…I mean Count"

The stately Italian gracefully clicked his heels and interrupted.

"Please…I am not pretentious of my birthright or the estate of my family in Florence. You may call me, "Ettore."

That could never be! The girls would not strip their countryman of his dignity with such familiarity. He would always be called, "The Count," when he was not around and Count Bertolucci when he was present.

And the girls used his title to their advantage. On one occasion, Carmella was threatened with termination if she did not work on the Count's special order. It would have meant coming in on Saturday morning and working until the evening hours. That would never be for any of the girls, who religiously attended the confraternity dances held on Saturday nights in the basement of the church.

One Thursday, as the girls were readying to leave the shop, Julius singled out Carmella and called her into his office demanding that she and one or two of the other girls come in on Saturday.

"You girls have to work or your canned, understand?" came the angry demand from Julius. Tears began to stream down Carmella's face and she ran out of his office.

It was Santina who came up with an idea. Her neighbor, Frankie Tarrone, called the shop on Friday afternoon posing as the Count's brother. He informed the clothier that his brother was sweet on all of the girls and wanted them to come to the airport and have dinner with him when he landed.

"He's crazy for your five workers and especially likes the "little one...Che cosa? Ahhh you call her, Carmella!" He announced convincingly.

"But...but...tell the Count, the girls need to fill his order and they need to work on Saturday night," came Julius' nervous response.

"Work...I know my brother and he will be incensed if they are not at the airport. He told me he will take his business elsewhere to...to...

"Goldberg and Fine," whispered Santina, who was listening in to the whole conversation and feeding Frankie every word.

"Fine and Goldberg, ahh...ahh, Capisce!" he tried to echo.

Needless to say, the girls were at the dance that Saturday night.

"Buon giorno Signorinas...I too am pleased to meet you all," he spoke in eloquent tones at this, their first meeting.

If Josephina was not leaning against her table, she might have fainted for the beauty in this countryman's speech and demeanor. Santina caught her childish gaze and gently tapped her heel against her calf.

"Mr. Bertolucci is touring our facility to see if his company might use our professional services for his line of scarves," Neuremberg announced.

"FACILITY?" Santina challenged in her mind, thinking...*does he mean this dump*? The brothers were not worthy of his trust or commitment, but he could be assured that any goods that were cut by Aldo and sewn by the girls would be perfect.

"We take pride in our work and try our best," she called out.

"I can only ask for your best work...then my customers will confirm my confidence, Miss...miss..." he spoke, fetching for Santina's name.

"Santina, sir...Santina Calabrese,"

"Ah! Calabria! You are good people," he smiled as he spoke. Josephina stared at him as Santina continued to talk to him about the old country. Years later, she still fantasized about living in a castle with him.

Daily life at the little shop was difficult at times. When the heating system broke one cold February day, the girls all stood up and donned their coats.

"Where are you going? It's not time to leave!" bellowed Julius

"I, I, I'm cold...we're cold," came a stuttering reply from Adeline.

"What? It's a little chilly...work and you'll warm up," came the reply.

Antoinette braced and took charge, like she had never before.

"We are leaving! We are freezing and sitting at our machines is not going to heat us up," she challenged.

"Go and you don't have to come back, see!" he screamed as he eyed each of the girls. That was it! As they left the building they knew they were out of a job. Aldo was not there to support or join them as he was home sick.

They were quickly replaced with temporary help. Two days later Adeline received a phone call asking her to speak to the girls about returning to work. They met at the candy store and reviewed their options.

"Who does he think he is?" bellowed Antoinette.

"If we go back now we've got him!" answered Santina then continued. The brothers need us, right? We go back and demand pay for the past two days. Those are our terms...what do you all think?"

"That's unheard of...getting paid for no work?" questioned Carmella.

"We do it…we just do it! I tell Julius and we all stand firm. Is it agreed?" Santina countered.

"But what if…" Carmella started, but was again interrupted.

"No backing down…we do it…together! Come on!" Santina ordered the girls and waited as Josephina nervously puffed the last few drags of her red-lipstick stained cigarette. They followed their leader as she climbed the steep stairs to their work place and the main office.

"Yes?" announced Isadore, as if he hadn't requested their return.

"We're back and we need to settle something once and for all," Santina cried out, not knowing what her boss's reaction might be.

"Settle what? You get a little cold; you walk out of the door. Now you come begging for your job and want to tell us about *settling* something," Harry chimed in response.

"We've decided to give you notice that we are quitting at the end of the week," Santina boldly switched here tactic. The girls braced for a messy mass firing…no, RE-FIRING!

"Quit, you can't do that! You have to give two weeks notice," Isadore nervously spewed his words.

"We're leaving right now! Come on girls," Santina ordered and began to walk to the stairs.

"Okay, what do you want to settle," Harry nervously replied.

"We get paid for the last two days and we stay on the job. Take it or leave it," Santina responded. The girls all folded their hands and stood ridged in their tracks.

"Okay, okay!" answered Harry.

"Okay? Okay?" came the disagreeing and anxious reply from Isadore.

"Shut up, Isadore and tell the accountant to pay them," ordered Harry.

"You'll kill this business yet," called Isadore in anger as he picked up the phone.

The girls did find out that their replacements were office temps who couldn't even thread a needle! Had they known that…they might have asked for a raise! It took Santina two days to stop shaking, but she finally did and never again had to confront either of her bosses in such a manner.

Now years later, she could still visualize the girls sitting at their machines working day in and day out. From time to time they considered moving on and trying other work, but the security of their little paycheck could not be compromised with a gamble on a dream.

During those early years at the Neuremberg's, the girls would sometimes sit out at a local park during their lunch break and talk about their hopes and plans for the future. For the most part, they were typical girls with typical dreams...with harmless fantasies and great expectations.

However, there are different kinds of dreams...deep visions and thoughts that stalk and will not let the mind or soul rest until realized. Adeline had such a dream and hid it in her heart.

As a young girl, she often fantasized about being a nun in the Catholic Church. Both her mother and grandmother pressed her to enter the Daughter's of Divine Guidance. She had grown up in Grasmere on Staten Island and attended elementary school at St. Dorothy's. There she embraced her faith and watched with awe as her teachers walked across the lush, green campus dressed in their flowing habits.

When the May Day procession was announced at school, she begged her mother to buy a dozen roses to place before the statue of the Blessed Mother. When her mother announced they could not afford it, she saved her allowance and walked to the local florist around the corner from her apartment.

When she arrived in front of the counter and was asked what she wished to purchase, Little Adeline held out sixteen nickels, eleven dimes and twenty-one pennies.

"Can I buy a dozen roses with this?" she asked as she lined up the coins in order on the counter top.

The florist smiled and slid the coins across the glass counter top.

"And just who are these flowers for...your mother?" the merchant inquired.

"They're for my Blessed Mother!" she innocently replied.

"Blessed Mother?" he asked with a wrinkled brow.

"Yes, the Blessed Mother!" she repeated

"Blessed Mother? Hey, kid...I'm Jewish and every Jewish mother is blessed...which one do you want the flowers for?" he laughingly responded.

"You don't know who the REAL Blessed Mother is?" she asked.

"Who is to know this REAL blessed Mother...I'm Jewish!" he answered.

"What's Jewish?" Adeline questioned.

"What's Jewish, she asks Murray Dreblatt, the Florist, no less?" came his reply.

"Hey mister, I just want some roses...Do you got any?" she asked.

"For this change I have a rose...with a sprig of baby's breath and a sheet of tissue paper," he answered.

"I'll take it, but you have to wrap it in that toilet paper stuff and put some of that little white grass around it so it will look pretty," Adeline added.

"Everyone is a florist!" The merchant smiled and wrapped the single rose with all the loving care one would use for such an innocent request.

On the day of the May procession, Adeline woke early in the morning to a thunderstorm that threatened to cancel the celebration. In the downpour, the little church-woman donned a yellow raincoat; high rubber boots an umbrella and ventured off to school. The festival was cancelled and rescheduled for the next day. Not hampered by the pouring rains, little Addie escaped during lunch and walked to the center of the campus lawn where she opened the metal fasteners of her raincoat and pulled out a now wilted single rose and placed it at the feet of the statue.

It was while she worked for the Neurembergs that one day she told the girls about her "calling."

"Are you crazy?" Antoinette chided.

"No, I'm not crazy...I just have this feeling inside!" Adeline answered

"A feeling? You feel something? I get a feeling this city should stop bank robbers, but I'm not going to become a cop," Antoinette challenged.

"It's different than being a cop. It's being married to God and helping others with their problems," Adeline answered.

"You never mentioned this before!" Santina called to her tenderly.

"I made up my mind last night while I was lying in bed. My mother is supposed to call today and find out all about it for me,"

Her mother did find out and three months later the girls took her out for a "last supper."

During the next sixteen months they pined for their friend, wrote weekly and hoped for the best. But on one brief visit home, Adeline confided that she wasn't sure she should take her final vows because her father was ill and the family needed to be supported. But there was something else that she had to deal with as well!

It was a brisk November morning when she again appeared at the office of the two Neuremberg Brothers and asked for her old job. They told her she could start the next day and without much explanation, she rejoined the girls and once again took her place at her old sewing desk. They never spoke about it much and didn't press her for the *real* reasons for coming out of the nunnery.

The real reason included a man. No, not just a man, but a priest.

Young John Mark Weston also felt called to the ministry and began his ministerial studies just after he graduated from Columbia. He casually met Adeline at a wedding and a bond was formed. Then they began to write to each other. The letters were simple...until they began to touch each other's very soul with words of spiritual purpose and human feeling. As it turned out, they didn't realize there was a thin line between the two. First, there was an appreciation for all that was beautiful and good. Then their familiarity brought them to a point of no return, when each confessed their most intimate sin: his desire for the touch of a woman and her attraction to his "tenderness."

They met again, quite by accident, in Newport, Rhode Island...he on vacation and she at a retreat. Late one night they walked around the old Viking Hotel and into the streets of the sleeping city. They were both in civilian clothes and somehow the absence of their religious attire led to an absence of their conscience. Adeline stood motionless when the young priest pressed his lips against hers and each released the adopted spiritual vows to the human passion both were feeling. One kiss was all they shared on that quiet evening. When the train pulled from the station the next morning, Adeline decided that she must return home...to her family and the promise of a life that would yield a husband and a family. John Mark Weston left the priesthood shortly thereafter and the two never corresponded again. It was a moment in time that had its virtue...but consequences far beyond that which either could bear...or fully understand at the time.

It wasn't sinful act that could not be forgiven, but it did reveal the true conscience and conviction of their calling to the church.

Then, just when everyone thought she'd be the old maid of the group, a man came into her life. It wasn't the usual course for meeting a man as her mother invited her husband's friend to come from Italy and spend a few weeks.

The idea of meeting a fine young man intrigued Adeline and she agreed to join her father and welcome him at the docks on one of Manhattan's piers.

What disembarked was quite different from what she saw in an old scratched photo he had sent months before. Standing before her was a man...her senior by at least fifteen years, fully bearded and dirty from his long voyage. His passport read PEASANT. He was poor and frail. Adeline's father snatched up his bags and walked ahead of her and the newcomer. She exchanged a few words with him, but for the most part, the greeting was brief. Later that evening, all shaved and cleaned, a rather stately and distinguished man sat at the end of the table conversing in his native tongue with her father. Why argue, she thought? If he was a good man, she'd probably marry him. It was all up to Papa. He would know a *good man* and that's all she wanted...a good man. They were married three months later and through the years had eight children...five girls and three boys: Rosie, Edith, Alba, Adeline, Anna, Joey, Johnny and Jimmy.

When the last child was born, her mother took her down to the doctor's office and demanded he "tie her tubes." If she hadn't engaged the procedure, she might have had eight more children!

But the advent of new babies was often overshadowed by death. As the years passed, Santina stood over the coffin of her aunts, uncles, brothers, sisters and cousins.

Of all the events circling the lives of the five girls, no time was more precious and more devastating than WW II. The war brought the girls to the realization that they really did not control their destinies, it was the most sobering period in their lives for it was the first time they all faced the death of people their age and younger. Yes, the old people died and there were accidents, but war... WAR made its own rules and timeline for the taking of life.

Death encountered each of them...one at a time.

Santina Fortunato woke one morning to an unfamiliar knock on her door. It was too early for the newspaper boy demanding payment for delivery and the mail was usually delivered at 2:00 pm. Her world was ordered and set in routine. The knock on the wooden storm door was loud and she feared her husband would be roused. It had a kind of staccato rhythm - surely from a firm and confident hand. It was a knock that would never be forgotten.

Santina moved quickly down the stairs and found her way to the front entrance. First she looked through the little peep-hole in the door, then without fear, opened the lock. Standing before her were three soldiers. SOLDIERS! Why were they calling at her home? What mistake had they made so early in the morning. Surely they meant to knock on the Pirandello Family, who lived three houses away. Joe and Angie's son, Giancarlo had shipped out a year before and was due to return home any day. But the visit wasn't for the Pirandello family. Three young men faced off and one addressed her formally.

"Mrs. Fortunato, We have an official communication from the United States Navy."

Santina stared at the three and pondered. What message did they bring? She carefully opened the envelope and slowly read each line. The words had no mercy as they pierced her heart. Her cousin Alessandro was missing in action over some remote Island in the Pacific. During that year the young soldier had buried both parents and having no brothers or sisters - Santina was the next of kin.

The three soldiers saluted, turned and left the yard. Their job was done and as official couriers, knew nothing more regarding the matter. She watched as they marched out to the yard and into the street. For a second she was angry that they were there in uniform and her cousin was trapped on some Island...somewhere in the middle of the Pacific. What gave them the right to be stationed on these sacred shores as her cousin was dropped from a parachute on some desolate beach. Then her anger faded and sadness filled her. Santina folded the letter and turned to enter the kitchen.

The house was quiet...her husband sleeping and her children away with their grandmother. She prepared coffee and listened as it began to perk and thought of all the things that could have happened to her cousin. All conjecture was in vain...she only knew that he was missing. Perhaps if it had been anyone other than Alessandro, she might have passively processed the whole affair until he had been found. But Alessandro was a gentle boy who loved her, not only as a cousin...but a friend. They shared the same birthday...but twenty years apart. Santina moved about as if in a stupor.

"What did you get?" asked her husband as he suddenly appeared, reaching for a cup in the cabinet.

"Alessandro is missing," Santina replied.

Silence followed and finally in quiet, but angry tones, her husband spoke.

"I don't know what to think. Why don't they take me...I'm old and finished," he remarked.

"They take these boys because they are boys. They have no life behind them and none before...that is why they take them. Boys don't ask questions, they don't think about the enemy as you do. You have lived too long, Vito...you know the pain of death and you would think too much if the enemy came upon you. In war, you cannot think with passion and humanity," Santina wisely answered.

"You want some coffee?" he asked.

Santina did not answer, but a piping hot cup of coffee was placed in front of her. Three months later, a pair of soldiers again appeared at her door and presented her with another letter. Alessandro's body was found in a ravine on an Island with a name Santina could not pronounce. No other details were given. Several months later a box containing his personal belongings appeared. Among them were Santina's four letters and a bracelet...the one she gave him for graduation. She turned it over to read the inscription she had engraved.

Al

Love always,

Sant

She remembered the day she presented it to him and watched as he fixed it to his left arm and recalled saying, "Wear it in good health." After all, that is what you were supposed to say when you gave a piece of jewelry to someone. Now he would be forever free from the cruelty and sickness in the world. Santina sometimes thought that good people were taken from this world by God to spare them from things to come. Who knows, she thought? The broken-hearted Seamstress brought the bracelet to her keepsake box, kissed it and placed it among the other treasures she held dear. But Santina was not alone in her sorrow.

Carmella never imagined that her boy Vinny Jr. would not return from the service. He was the smart one in the family...like his father, she would tell people. Months before, the entire family watched as he boarded the large aircraft carrier on Manhattan's Westside with the other neighborhood boys and set out for an unidentified port. The youthful face and muscular body promised the world a prize, thought Carmella.

"Ma, don't worry...I'll be ok," he said the evening before his departure.

"You are a boy!" exclaimed his mother.

"Ma, I'm eighteen!" he declared.

"Leave him alone...he is a man...he'll be all right," Vinny Sr. called to her.

"Why did you let him sign up? "Carmella began to cry.

"Easy...easy!" he responded.

"*Easy*, he says...a boy is eighteen going off to war and his father says ea*s*y," she cried out.

The next day they found themselves on the shore waving goodbye to their firstborn son. How could they know he would never return home again?

Years later, at night when she was alone, Carmella would stand outside of his bedroom door and listen to the silence. Then her mind would escape to the past and she would see him playing baseball or digging in the backyard. How precious were the shadows of the mind … but oh how cruel they were to the heart.

For Antoinette, the war brought more sorrow than she could bear at the time. Her uncle…two months her junior, was found among a group of soldiers on the shores of a deserted beach in the pacific.

Her mother and grandmother had been pregnant at the same time. In those days, babies brought great joy to families and it was common for six to twelve siblings join hands for a family picture… uncles, aunts and cousins all within five years of age. Guido was one of the gang in that group. An uncle, he was just a year and a half older then Antoinette. He was cute, wearing his pegged pants and always chomping on a piece of gum. His slicked-back hair gave him the proper identity among his peers and Antoinette adored him. He was in her bridal party and she was in his. As infants, they were breast fed by whoever was available at the time…mother, grand-mother or aunt. Family was family and knew no boundaries for love and care.

The devoted cousin found herself in deep depression for months after the funeral. They buried him somewhere on Long Island…far away from the city. It was a place for soldiers and thousands were buried there. It was quiet and still… and while she never returned to the gravesite, she thought of him every day of her life.

Josephina also bore the heart burden of loss due to the perils of war. When her cousin Connie brought around her new guy, Carmine, to meet the family, how could she know that someday he would be taken from them so soon after they were married…and, so young. Men were supposed to die before their wives… in their sleep or even after a long illness…and always when they were old. Women were to follow…months or a few years later. Carmine was a native of Palermo and came to America at the suggestion and invitation of the tenants who lived upstairs. A tailor, Josephina and her husband set him up in business on Bay Street in Stapleton. The sign outside of the door was simple and to the point, *Expert Tailor*. His customers loved him and at twenty-six he was indeed an expert. But the army did not survey his vocational credentials...only his age and health. Months before he pulled out, Connie gave birth to twins...two little girls...Maria and Victoria. They joined a sixteen month old baby brother...Mario. Two nights before he was to return home for a twenty four hour leave, the transport he was in was hit by enemy fire. The little damsels would never know their father. Years later...in another war, she was to lose her two sons.

And Adeline was not spared the tragedy of the war. Her younger brother-in-law, Filippo was found to have no vision in one eye, so he was exempt. But his exemption did not preclude him from work at an arms factory at the Brooklyn Navy Yard. Ironically, while he was exempt due to vision, he was an expert welder. One day he stepped on some metal and it pierced his working boots. He spoke nothing of it at home and endured the growing pain. Finally, when he could bear it no longer, he was taken to the hospital and within a week died of gangrene infection. He left his family of four with nothing more than a box of tools and one week's pay. Marianna, his wife went to live with Adeline and her family. It was supposed to be for a few weeks. Twenty-three years later, she was still the tenant in their fourth floor apartment. But the horror of war revisited them again when another relative died in Vietnam.

Each of the girls had faced the perils of war in their own way. While they would have given their own lives in exchange for their loved ones, there is no bartering for life when war is declared and young men announce that they will serve...whatever the cost.

On one occasion they openly shared the pain and sorrow of their losses. It was late one night, when Josephina suggested they cool off at the harbor and take a quick trip to Manhattan and back on the Staten Island ferry. There, under the open skies, each unfolded their stories and quietly wept, while staring at the sky.

Santina looked at the casket of Angelina Caruso and saw her friends as one by one they knelt and prayed. Good Catholics remembered their dead family members and friends and prayed diligently that the All Mighty would show mercy on them. She grinned, thinking that there was nothing about Angelina that would keep her from a fine house in heaven. And, God could be assured of one thing...the house of Angelina Caruso would be clean.

Her quiet thoughts were interrupted when she saw Giorgio Camarota bow to pray. Angelina Caruso's neighbor for more than fifty years was sure to pay his last respects. If it were not for the Caruso Family, he would have been sent back to Catania in Sicily. It wasn't that he didn't have necessary money to fund his existence until he could get a job, but a foolish mistake he made a few weeks after he entered the country.

At a local gin mill, he made friends with some countrymen who offered him some *easy money* if he would do them a favor. All he had to do was to wait in his car on a certain corner at a certain time. They would meet him and he would drive them to the airport. It sounded innocent and simple and although he had only driven a car a few times, he was willing to help them. After all, they were his compadres and the code among Italians was to always be ready to help a countryman.

At exactly 2:30 pm, the innocent immigrant was faithfully waiting for his riders to appear. Within a few minutes he witnessed them running toward the car from a side street. Massimo and Antonio, by name, jumped into the rear seat.

"Go...go!" they spoke in feverish commands.

"Si, si," answered Giorgio as he sped away into the flow of traffic almost hitting cars as he found his place in the flow.

Two months later he was arrested when the two Compadres identified him as the mastermind of a bank robbery they said they had passively and reluctantly participated in on that fateful day.

Angelina took a small loan out at the same bank that was robbed and paid a lawyer to defend him. At the trial he sat silent as the judge and jury listened to the witnesses. No one was able to identify Giorgio and he was about to be set free when he sarcastically called out and mimicked the judge. He was incensed by the disrespect and about to sentence him for being an accessory to the crime when Angelina jumped to her feet and pleaded with the judge to let her countryman come into her home and under her supervision. Reluctantly, he agreed and he was placed in her care...on probation.

He bent over the casket and kissed his benefactor and touched her hand in respect of their life-long friendship. It was Angelina and her husband who also loaned him the two thousand dollars to open an old shuttered gasoline station in Huntington, out on Long Island. Occasionally, on Sundays, the family would pile into their Chevrolet Woody station wagon, board the ferry to Brooklyn and take the long ride out to see him. He would open the station and fill their car with gasoline and spend hours sharing and learning what was going on in their lives. One Sunday in June, when their son Andrew had just graduated from Port Richmond High School, he stayed on in Huntington and remained there as an apprentice to Giorgio. It was to be a temporary arrangement, until he had learned the trade. He never returned to Staten Island.

Now on in years and retired, Giorgio respectfully walked to the row of chairs in front of the casket and greeted his adopted cousins. Had it not been for their mother, he would surely have spent a lifetime struggling to fit into society. He wept like a child with a broken heart.

The stately Italian woman lay in the polished coffin and Santina reasoned that she had lived a good life...giving of herself to her family and friends and an immigrant named...Giorgio.

And Santina also had wonderful memories of helping others. In 1942, a cousin from Sicily wrote asking if she could visit America. She sent Santina a picture and a long letter describing her intentions while visiting, but little did Santina know that the major intention was to meet a rich American and relocate. Santina had helped numerous friends and relatives come and settle in America. Sadly, many became victims of a dream and sometimes those who dream did not factor the cruel realities of forging a life in a strange land, far from the shores of their birth. Dreamers had to yield their energies to daily survival when they learned the streets were not paved with gold!

Palma Tangianno walked down the plank of the freighter toward Santina with a big smile on her face. That wasn't the only thing that was big. She weighed no less than three hundred and fifty pounds and carried two small packages filled with all of her worldly possessions. Cousin Palma looked like something out of an old time silent movie, except she wasn't silent. The picture she sent didn't even closely resemble her and Santina later learned it was indeed a picture of a cousin... Gloria Maria...Palma's sister.

For the next two weeks she did nothing but talk about her life and experiences as a cook in a castle in Florence. The truth was that she was a dishwasher at a second rate hotel near Bologna. By her size, Santina concluded her cousin must have been paid fifty cents a day and all she could eat. And eat she did. Santina could hardly keep up with the daily demand for pasta, cheese and bread.

But something unbelievable happened to Palma. She met an old man who was loaded with money, married him and had four children. To no ones surprise, she outlived her first husband and married his brother...who was the next of kin. Two children later, he was hit by a bus and died. Two husbands later, she died of complications of diabetes. Santina was at her bedside that day and kissed her gently as she slipped into a coma and passed away.

Santina Fortunato's life had been filled with many cousins, friends and neighbors, but Palma had a special placed in her heart. Her successes in marrying rich time after time did not shelter her from the consequences of her ignorance. She died penniless due to questionable investments and Santina, who sheltered her during that first year in America...had to pay for her final shelter.

Vito Fortunato was an understanding husband who tolerated Santina's generosity and foolish trust in others. He loved her passionately, but more importantly... he liked her as well. Yes, he loved her, but there was more to their union then the longevity of years or the permanence they found in the bond of marriage. He adored everything about her.

It was in 1949 when she received a phone call from someone identifying himself as a relative. Rinaldo Carrara was his name and Santina agreed to let him visit for a few hours after disembarking from his boat. When she inquired if he had a place to stay, he said he was going to a local hotel until he could get an apartment. Santina called Vito and explained the situation. He agreed to let him stay for a few days.

On the eve of the second night, Rinaldo didn't return home until after midnight.

"And where were you tonight?" demanded Vito.

"I go to see a show," he lied.

"The movie ends at ten thirty, so where have you been?" came the second question.

"I visit a friend," his houseguest exclaimed.

"Who do you know?" Vito questioned.

"You aska too many questions," Rinaldo angrily answered.

The two men were staring at each other in anger when Santina broke the silence demanding that everyone retire for the evening.

"And how do you know he is a relative?" questioned Vito as he lay next to Santina on their bed.

"He is a relative," explained Santina.

"I don't like anything about him," said Vito as he turned away from his wife in disgust.

"He will be leaving on Saturday. Be patient, Vito," came Santina's reply.

The next day they learned why their countryman had been late the night before. Vito read the newspaper out loud and put the pieces together for Santina.

"It says that a bar was robbed by a man carrying a pistol. He shot the man and he is in critical condition at the hospital. Listen to this, the man spoke with an accent and they think he is from Italy or Sicily. I know who this man is!" announced Vito.

"And who do you think it is?" demanded Santina.

"Who? Who? The stranger in my house…that's who!" Vito fired back.

"Ehh!" Santina barked.

Sure enough, Rinaldo was easily identified by the bar's patrons that night.

"I'm not paying a penny for his bail," barked Vito.

"He's family!" begged Santina.

"Family? He's a crook!" bellowed Vito.

Again, Santina was suckered in and paid for his bail.

"He will leave town unless I chain him down," promised Vito.

"No, he's a good boy. He just made a mistake," Santina stated.

The only mistake that was made was the expense of the bail. Rinaldo disappeared to South Jersey and was never caught. Rumor had it that he gone back to Sicily, but Vito found out that Santina's "relative" a known thief in his own country and would have been extradited, if caught. Vito never let Santina forget about the money they loaned and lost that day trying to help their mystery guest.

"Crucify me!" she would bawl at him when he mentioned the incident.

"Ehh!" he would reply.

Santina turned to the sound of crying that came from the back of the funeral parlor. The voice was not familiar and she wondered who it was that could not contain their grief. Then she identified the accent. It was Caterina Bosco, one of Angelina's in-laws by a baby born out of wedlock. They were neighbors when Caterina's daughter, Patsy, first met Louie, Angelina's first born.

They met at in high school during their sophomore year. By their senior year, they had brought a little girl into the world and created havoc among the families, each blaming the other for the "accident." Till the day she died, the families never got together...not even for a cup of coffee. For the kids, it was a living hell and a lifetime of grief each time there was a get-together.

Santina resigned that the tears being shed at the rear of the room were those of repentance...for an unforgiving relationship between two people. The union of their children should have bound them, but they chose to spend nearly twenty-five years separate and angry at each other.

"Santina!" Caterina called as she made her way through the isle to her side.

"Caterina, how are you?" asked Santina.

"How am I?" She questioned herself, then continued...She's gone! That's how I am...I thought she would live forever. Now that she is no longer here, I only wish we could have been friends. I used to tell myself that I would think this way if she died first, now look at me," Caterina spoke in a tearful voice.

"Yes, we all wish she was here. She was a good woman and we will all miss her," Santina said consolingly.

Caterina lowered her head and wept quietly in Santina's arms with the other girls looking on. Carmella reached over to pat Caterina's shoulder.

"Don't be hard on yourself Caterina," she spoke as she continued to touch her head.

"If she was here, I would ask her to forgive me for my foolishness...my anger," the woman replied.

"It is time to move on now...to forgive yourself and let go," Santina wisely spoke. She found a seat and stared ahead at the coffin.

Santina was beginning to watch her old friends pass on one at a time. Each had a lifetime of memories attached to their union and as each chapter closed, she knew that someday the final chapter would be written for her and that she would lie in a flower-filled room with people talking, laughing and remembering.

Perhaps that is what life was all about...doing things to record and measure the past. That was the one of the things she struggled with in her mind...the passing of time. Often she would reflect on the years as if they truly were chapters in book. She measured her life by the things she did and wished she had done. Sometimes at night when the world seemed to pause and wait for her next thought, she would engage the past and future as if they were one and the same. Perhaps there was something yet for her to do...people to meet, places to visit and something to be accomplished.

One time she confessed to Adeline that the most difficult person she had to deal with in her life was...Santina Calabrese Fortunato!

"You are too hard on yourself, Santina!" Adeline would tell her.

"I don't know how to be hard on anyone else," she would reply

Santina Fortunato had learned to stay busy and consumed with something...every moment of her life.

In her closet, lay dozens of things to mend and knit. The need to create or fix things ruled her days. She thought how important it was for each person to fit into the world without changing it and ultimately saying or doing something that would not be forgotten. Every life should have purpose. No one should live and not leave something. While others left wealth, property or title, she wanted to leave her family something more. Yes, she must leave her reputation...a good woman who lived a good life!

As she stared at the body of this old friend, she contemplated the remainder of her own life. Would there be five or ten years more for her? Could the remaining years be meaningful and pertinent to the life of her family? For what would she be remembered? And then again, is a person to be remembered at all or is it best that the remnants of her life be sold, discarded, laid to rest and forgotten? What could a simple seamstress really leave behind, except a silent presence?

While lost in her thoughts, the local priest entered the room and greeted those who openly and quietly grieved.

The funeral director walked to the front of the room and solemnly requested that everyone be seated. When the room quieted, the priest walked to the front of the casket and spoke. He couldn't have been over thirty and here he was attempting to reflect on the accomplishments of the dead lying behind him.

What could he know about her? They were strangers...from different parts of the world and another time. His was a world of modern convenience! She was a mere reflection of a disappearing world.

"Our dear sister was a woman of faith," he began.

What could he possibly know about her, except she was a Catholic woman in his parish? Could his own thirty years have told him about her world...her problems and her fears. Could he know about the miscarriages death of her daughter at age ten, who innocently walked across the street to visit grandma and was struck by a speeding truck? Would he be able to reflect on the moments of struggle when her husband was laid off from work or the depression years when she scraped together a meal from two potatoes an egg and day-old bread?

"She knew the love of her family and friends!" He continued

Of course she knew love of family and friends, thought Santina. What he didn't know was the rejection Angelina felt from her mother-in-law, who went to her grave cursing the day her son married the foreigner from another village. The petty differences in culture of the two towns amounted to a lifetime of verbal punishment.

"And her devotion to the church was boundless!" he added.

The Church? Where was her church when her first husband of three months ran out on her and moved to a far off place called Ohio?" Her church was there all right. It was ready to forgive her for

74

the sin of her husband, providing she cough up five hundred and fifty dollars for an annulment. In spite of this, the young priest should only know how obediently she held to her church's teaching.

Santina remembered the night Angelina came to her door, frantic with the news that her god-son had died while in battle. She sat with her for hours on the back porch.

"And what did you do for her, Santina? What could you say to comfort her?" her husband questioned as he lay next to her in bed.

"I said nothing!" She responded.

"What did you do on the porch for so long?" he again questioned.

"I held her hand we cried together," she whispered to him in the dark.

Santina was not one to think she could do anything to change the heart of another person, but was always there to laugh, dream or weep with them.

"Let us pray for our sister as she awaits her heavenly reward," the kindly priest continued.

Santina scanned the room to see the faithful bow and pray. She wondered if any of them had ever had a second thought of her during the years she spent on earth. Now they all reverently bowed their heads and repeated the incantation of their spiritual leader.

Such reverence was novel because it only existed when they were called upon to seek the Almighty God for something. Santina was sure they begged His intervention when they were gambling or when either Duke or Mickey was up at bat. One would have difficulty finding the true and devoted Catholic at a baseball field. There on the 'sacred diamond' of play, more prayers were sent upward then at any other time. Now the group was asked to spend a moment and beseech the Father for tolerance in the life of their friend.

The priest prayed earnestly that Angelina would be ushered into heaven and that she would be forgiven for her sins and transgressions. Compared to others, thought Santina, her dear friend was already a saint...one worthy of special treatment up on high.

"She's with my mamma," whispered Carmela as she lowered herself on one of her knees to pray.

"Yes," smiled Santina. She would see all those who had gone on before. She would tell them all about what was going on down on earth. Again, Santina thought of all her friends…those she would not see in the years to come. One by one they were passing. She had lived through four wars, epidemics, and the cruelty of life on earth. She would be spared a world that was full of gaps and inconsistencies … like another civilization…so different from the world in which she grew up. Angelina Caruso would never see the hundreds of children who would come from the seed of her husband, nor would she be able to help them with their struggles and pain.

It wasn't that Santina thought that life did not have its purpose and beauty. Oh no! She loved life, but knew death ended the struggle and the pain of living in a world that dared you to exist amidst its impassionate darts…thrown one at a time.

Out of the corner of her eye, she saw Carmela unravel the plastic on a Chicklet box and held her hand out as two square pieces found their way into her hand. She too, caught Santina with her eyes open and offered her the box…but she nodded *no* in response.

"In the name of the Father and of the Son and of the Holy Ghost, Amen!" the priest finished his prayer.

A moment later he exited the formal room bidding good night to those in his path. The truth of it all is that he never really knew his parishioner for he had just arrived at the church weeks before.

The local church had also changed. Santina remembered the statues and massive pews that furnished her church. She had brought her children for baptism and communion and watched as her daughters walked the long isle as she had done years before. While other institutions had changed, the church seemed to have a kind of stability. At least to the eye, things appeared to be the same. But where hundreds once gathered, the pews, of late, were barren and the choir was a pathetic remnant of the past. In the old days, the vast concrete structure echoed with the sounds of powerful voices. She observed that people didn't seem to sing much anymore…in or out of church. The love songs of the past now gave way to the harsh psychedelic lights and sounds of an era that seemed to want nothing to do with the past.

Santina had watched the world change. She could still hear the gay and happy songs of the Big Bands and romantic crooners of the forties and remembered dancing to the music of Frank Sinatra and

Vaughn Monroe. These had lasted through the decades and linked one generation with the next. Today, the young people seemed to disdain the sweet melodic refrains. The movies had also changed. The simple stories that were usually birthed in good books and rewritten for the screen were displaced by vulgar and irreverent themes whose goal seemed only to titillate and frighten, rather than entertain.

Yes, the world she knew had changed dramatically. There seemed to be no link to the early years and while her grandchildren yearned to learn of her past, they quickly bored with the details her life and sometimes left her mid-sentence and alone in her memories.

There was one memory...one piece of her past that she would never reveal to her children or grandchildren. It was a minor infraction that made her feel stained and less than honorable. Sometimes the small events in life...the little mistakes transcend all the good that comes before and follows.

It happened one night when she was fifteen years old. She accompanied two of her friends to the local drugstore and sat for an ice cream soda. It was to be an innocent evening of talk and laughter.

When one of the girls suggested that they look at the make-up counters, Santina walked down to view the lipstick display. She reached for a bright red tube when out of the corner of her eye she witnessed one of her girlfriends take a pressed powder box and place it in her purse. She looked over at Santina, who was opening the tube and called, "Take it, Santee!"

Santina clutched the make-up in her hand and, without thinking, quickly buried it in her purse.

"Let's go!" the other girl called as she turned to get out of the store. In a second they had exited the store, goods in hand and began to run down the street to the park. There, Santina sheepishly opening her pocketbook and showed her contraband to her girl friends.

During the evening the conversation was light and carefree; but when she returned home to her room, Santina could not get the deed out of her mind. Never in her life could she remember such guilt and mental pain. It was only twenty five cents and even had the money in her purse to pay for it...but she had succumbed to the temptations of youth.

Finally, she fell asleep and found a temporary peace. In the morning her first thoughts were of the theft. She thought about it all day long and wondered what to do to rectify the deed, but no closure followed. She was a thief...if only for a worthless item. The reality of her petty crime ran deep and for the rest of her life, every time she placed a shade of deep red lipstick on her lips, she thought of the loneliness and emptiness of that night and the days that followed her youthful folly.

She never revealed her youthful indiscretion or how she felt as a result. Santina carried the pressure of those days for the rest of her life. How silly, she once told herself? Why didn't she bring the tube back to the store and place it on the shelf? Years later she reasoned...youth has little commonsense and even less ingenuity.

But she did learn something from the incident...she never again took anything without paying full price. Yes, there were things she thought to keep to herself and this had to be one of them. Perhaps it was false pride to escape the scrutiny or shame of her children...or a desire to keep her credibility in a world where her children saw little...if any at all in those people around them.

"Did Madeline find out if she is pregnant?" Carmela questioned as she broke through Santina's unsettling thoughts.

Santina's granddaughter thought she was going to have her first baby and everyone awaited the doctor's report. At the turn of the century families were filled with babies. It was part of the future... the promise of an extension into the new country. First generation Italians suffered under the harsh scrutiny of the Irish and struggled for an identity. Now, a generation later, the families were smaller and marriages came later on in life. She remembered the necessity of marrying and it was not uncommon for girls to walk down the isle at fifteen or sixteen. The expectation was that you married your own kind...an Italian...older and smarter. But Santina knew her children would not hold to the tradition and most did marry out of their culture. Two of the marriages did end in divorce and Vito swore it was because they didn't marry their own kind...Italians. He also swore that the younger children and grandchildren would not escape the traditions if he had anything to say about it. Love, however, was not able to discern the national background of an individual and knew no prejudice. Even Vito came to accept the other cultures...but always reluctantly.

He also learned that love moved beyond the petty intolerance of color and race. When his daughter Elizabeth announced that a fine young man had asked her to the junior prom, Santina took her out to buy a new dress. At the affair her daughter danced with a Negro boy and all hell broke loose two days later when it was reported to Vito by one of his co-workers.

"He's a malanzana!" he barked at Santina

"Why do you make such a big thing out of this! She only danced with the boy," Santina explained.

"That's how it starts!" came the reply.

"How what starts?" Santina fired back.

"You know what I mean...the next thing they go boom, boom!" Vito argued.

"What do you mean, boom, boom?" Santina fired back.

"Santina Calabrese...you know what I mean by, boom, boom!" he challenged her, calling out her maiden name to emphasize his point.

Nothing came of the brief encounter, but that did not stem the tide of prejudice.

Through the years Santina had learned to put aside her prejudices and accept people of all backgrounds. She recalled the time when she faced off with a German lady who came to work at Neuremberg's.

The tension was felt almost immediately when Santina was asked to explain the operation of the sewing machine to her.

"Vee have like dis in Munich!" the woman explained.

"But this is a new model and you have to operate it with..." Santina began.

"Vee have like dis in Munich!" she repeated.

That was the beginning of a war at the shop...because she did NOT have like "dis" in Munich and broke two machines.

"Those Germans thought they were going to take over the world till our boys got over there and told them different," Vito would proudly argue.

"Everyone thinks they can take over the world," Santina would reply.

"Heinz, one of my painters, had his boys enrolled in a German school to learn the language…he was all ready to have Hitler run this country," Vito argued.

The depression and wars that they had lived through made them suspicious of foreigners…just as their parents were suspect when they came to America. Santina told herself that she was too old to hold to such thinking. It was a time to love everyone and run from the pettiness that separates people.

The German woman would look at the five girls in distain. They were all second generation Americans and did not have an accent to separate them from the natives. Sometimes they would talk about her and argue that she was coarse and unfriendly. Santina would smile at their angry remarks and speak kindly of her.

"Remember, she is new to this country and to her we are the strangers. She must be lonely and frightened. Think about her…all alone in a little apartment at night…struggling to read a newspaper with words she does not understand, listening to a radio with foreign tongues and humor she does not understand."

The girls would listen in silence. Santina's wisdom truly made her their senior. They would often go to her with questions about what they should do about this or that. Their quandaries were never really life shattering, but the thoughtful words of their "Big Sister, Santina," were enough to answer their questions and concerns. But she also had to exercise that special wisdom in her own life…and, while Vito was a good provider, he often left the big decisions to her.

One of the biggest decisions of her life came when she located a house that needed a considerable amount of repair and could be purchased cheaply. The bank was offering the house at auction and while she knew little about the process, showed up to place her one and only bid.

Assembled in front of the county clerk's office was a group of people ready to compete for the little house on old Van Duzer Street. She was just twenty-eight years old at the time and looked nineteen. Those assembled around her were coarse and looked as though they would pounce on anyone who tried to outbid them. Santina begged Vito to participate, but he would have nothing to do with the process. It was out of their financial range, he would say in so many words.

"And how will you pay for this castle you are going to win? We have a nice little house now and I paid your father for the loan," he challenged.

"We need a bigger house now that I am pregnant again," she answered.

After waiting for more than two hours, several of the bidders had already left the site and Santina stood among those remaining to garner the prize.

A rather undistinguished man appeared on the steps and announced the auction would begin in a few minutes. He spent a good deal of time explaining the property and the terms. While he yet spoke, two more people left the site and only three bidders were left standing next to Santina.

"Opening bid is one thousand five hundred dollars...do I have a bid?" came the first words to start the auction.

Santina had exactly five thousand three hundred dollars allocated for her bidding.

"Now, I have thirty-five hundred, I have thirty-five hundred!" the clerk echoed.

Santina watched as two more bidders left the site and further eyed them until they had reached the street and their respective cars.

Now Santina and one man remained to bid on the house.

"I have a bid of five thousand dollars....do I have five thousand one hundred?" he sang out to the two remaining bidders.

The man snapped to bid and raised a confident hand.

Santina's heart sank for she knew he could go higher...perhaps much higher then she could ever dream of bidding.

"Do I have five thousand three hundred?" the clerk called out, as if he too could raise the price much higher.

"Five thousand, three hundred dollars," Santina stammered.

"Five thousand and three hundred dollars! I have five thousand three hundred dollars!" the clerk repeated

Santina turned to her competitor and waited.

"Ah, the house isn't worth it. I'll wait for the next one, John," He announced...obviously knowing the clerk, who smiled and repeated the final bid.

"Going once, twice, sold for five thousand three hundred dollars," he called in completion.

Santina could hardly control her emotions. She grabbed the hand of the man and kissed it.

"Hey, lady…if I knew you were going to kiss me, I would have dropped out five minutes ago," he said as he smiled and waved his hand at the clerk.

Three months later, the Fortunato family walked up the steps of their new house. It was the biggest decision and gamble she had ever made…but one that would impact her family for years to come.

Through the years the neighbors and neighborhood had changed, but the Fortunato family had remained. Now, from the same window where she once watched her children playing…she saw the dirty streets and broken down cars cluttering the neighborhood. It was a sad sight, but where could she go. She absolutely refused to live with her children, knowing that they needed their privacy and she needed her quiet times. They begged her to sell the house, but she refused. Santina would argue that when people got old and their children moved them from their house…that such moving broke their spirit and their independence. Even their health failed.

"This is the house of your father and mother and I do not want to move to a strange place." Perhaps she was right. The dignity of self-sufficiency was necessary at all ages…but most important when you reached the older years.

Amidst the noise, she sat quietly in the funeral parlor lost in her own thoughts. The Seamstress had been to so many funerals of late and reasoned there were only a few of the older friends left. Yes, that was their designation…"old." But it meant more than an accounting of the years they had lived on earth. It was a term that captured the very essence of their life…rich in experience and insight into the world. These were people who were content with the simple necessities of life: a dish of pasta…a newborn baby… a visit from a friend! The old people…who could forget any of them - even though most were gone many years now? They were the most important people in a person's life…the stability of the family… the past that footed the present and future.

And…each one of them was a character in their own right…a little craziness and a lot of individuality. It left one thinking, *how could a person with so little earthly wealth, be so happy?* They had a limited formal education and most had never traveled beyond a few miles from their house. Yet if you held the highest degree offered at the local college, you still sought and respected their advice and wisdom.

Perhaps the most repeated expression in the Italian community was…*what do you think papa…mamma?* Their counsel and advice was a necessary confirmation that you were doing the right thing. It was a kind of blessing that was a necessary part of your life. The aunts and uncles were always there to partake in your future…even if it meant that you changed directions. Their advice was governed by a type of morality and goodness that was fast being replaced by a generation determined to live their life according to feeling; a generation that exchanged wisdom for psychology…the God in heaven for the gods on earth.

These days the kids rebelled against old fashioned common sense, thought Santina. Like most people she was one who loved to give her opinion…but in her case, only if asked. Her Aunt Anna Ruth operated on a different assumption. She felt it was her duty to impose her *recommendations* on others and enjoyed the words, *"I told you so,"* more than any others. She wanted to put her two cents in…even when someone asked…*a penny for your thoughts, aunt*!

On one occasion when a niece asked Aunt Anna Ruth what she thought of her latest boyfriend. She offered her opinion and warned the girl that the boy could not be trusted. The young girl asked how she knew and the Aunt said she saw something in his eye that told her.

"Malocchio!" she summed.

The *old evil eye* was a standby for her and most Italians feared the "mystic curse." Her niece had such faith in her that she broke up with the guy immediately. Come to find out, the poor kid had a glass eye and was the son of a very wealthy banker. She never forgave her for the bad advice because the young man went on to study medicine and became a veterinarian. She never married!

But there were others whose advice you wouldn't want to live without…those who lived unpretentiously and made no imposition on the family. They were always ready to help and guide and each had a kind of wisdom that you couldn't glean from a hundred years at college. Sometimes their insight was profound and so accurate that one would believe they had some kind of divine understanding of temporal matters.

She remembered Grandpa John who never said much...but was always there sitting and listening quietly. He was respectfully known as the *OLD MAN*. It was not spoken in a derogatory sense, but out of respect for his age and position in the family. He was Vito's grandfather, and while he was THE *old man* in the family, everyone called him *Papa*. He was unassuming and quiet in a way where you didn't know when he was around...or when he was missing.

On one occasion, after the wedding reception of Santina's daughter Christina, everyone said goodnight and went to their respective homes. Everyone, that is, except Papa! Somehow he was forgotten and when the family inventoried heads in the cars as they pulled into their driveways, they discovered that he had been left behind. A phone call confirmed he was there sitting quietly in front of the reception hall drinking a Schaefer Beer...his favorite.

That was Papa...part of the wonderfulness...the kind you loved and whose memory you desperately clung to when you sat quietly in the evening all alone or reminisced with the uncles, aunts and cousins at an occasional get-together.

They were the true "individuals" in society...bearing their own brand of uniqueness. Some of them were so *unique*...it brought tears to your eyes...the kind that come when you can't stop laughing!

At the wedding reception of Santina's daughter Maria, aunt Carina sat with the family as the local priest walked to the microphone to ask the blessing on the affair. The priest lowered his head, two hundred guests lowered their head and the entire room went silent. He began his prayer and because it wasn't loud enough for Aunt Carina to hear, she called out, "I can't hear what the hell he's trying to say!" The rest is a matter of record. Half the family cringed in embarrassment, while the other half went into to laughing frenzy. Surely the prayer must have been sincere and solemn... but no one heard it.

The amazing thing about these old people was their stability. For instance, no one ever got a divorce. The church and the inner community prohibited it. But there was even more to it than the obvious restraints. Their marriages were welded together with a passionate desire to survive. Yes, that's what they were, reasoned Santina...*survivors*!

It was not uncommon for couples to be married for fifty, sixty or seventy years. Santina's Uncle Massimo and Aunt Louise were married for seventy-two years when it was revealed that the man who married them on the boat coming over from Italy was not authorized to marry anyone. Through the years they had never been asked for a marriage certificate and no one had ever challenged their union. It was on Uncle Massimo's deathbed that he confessed to paying one of the ship's mates to impersonate the captain and perform the ceremony. He forged the marriage certificate stolen from the captain's desk on the night they left the ship. For over seventy years, Louise never knew she was not legally married.

Oh, there were stories...so many of them that Santina said one day she would write a book. In the case of her Uncle Massimo and Aunt Louise, there was little to question after so many years. There was also one other thing they would have had trouble explaining. During their seventy-two years, they had brought eleven children, twenty-seven grandchildren and seventy-six great grandchildren into the world. Were they all illegitimate? When Aunt Louise passed on, so did the secret of their marriage. Only a few family members were privy to the story...and each promised to take it to their graves.

There were many things that were *supposed* to be taken to the grave. The trouble with most families is that everyone had a secret and they were just dying to tell it to someone. Secrets that were supposed to go to the grave...definitely lived on. For instance, there was one female member of the family whose name was never mentioned in public. While it was supposed to be a secret, everyone knew the truth about *Cousin Rita*. But oh, the private conversations about her would light up a room...or two. She was just one of the cousins growing up with the rest of the family. She went to work as a typist, a skill she had learned while attending New Dorp High School. She graduated on June 28th and celebrated the Fourth of July on *New Dorp Beach* with her cousins. On July 5th she boarded the train and Staten Island Ferry and was transported off to Manhattan with dozens of other girls who graduated days before with her.

Few noticed the subtle changes in her personality, but as the months rolled on she seemed to mature and become more sophisticated. In two years time she was definitely a *woman of the world...* dressed in the latest fashions with make-up that was flawless.

During that time she moved out of her parent's home and took an apartment in Greenwich Village. At least that is what everyone thought. And to add to her story, she would complain that the apartment was very small and that she shared it with an older woman who also worked for the same mid-town firm. It all sounded very believable.

On one cold February night, after a family get-together, Cousin Frankie offered to drive her back to the city as he was en route to Connecticut. Once in the car, Cousin Rita gave him directions to a Park Avenue apartment. When his rather dated Ford pulled to the curb, a doorman opened the rear door, pulled a suitcase from the floorboard and extended a hand to the chauffeur's cousin. Frankie was literally in shock when he greeted her by name.

"Hello, Miss Furno...I do hope your trip was a pleasant one!"

Frankie's mouth was wide open with surprise as his cousin turned and blew a kiss.

"Our little secret, okay, Frankie?" she asked as she cocked her head and smiled.

Cousin Rita was the private guest of her boss and lived in luxury. She was employed at an office, but was provided with *extra benefits* for her work. Frankie knew never to say anything because he thought it would kill her parents; but it was a secret that her cousin could not shield. When her boss was indicted for embezzlement, standing by his side on the front page pictures was his *companion.* Guess who? Throughout the court proceedings it appeared they were inseparable and that a divorce from his wife would ensue.

Her family never spoke about it openly, but some of the uncles were to check on her from time to time.

"Disgraziata!" the old people would say!

"Puttana!" they would call out when her name came up in a conversation. Rita didn't marry her boss and never had children either.

But Santina knew her cousin was lonely and needed some family contact. She called to assure her that she loved her and wanted to keep in touch. Secretly, Santina would let her know when someone was born, married or died. And Rita was certain to receive a birthday card every year with a little note to let her know she was missed and loved. Every family had a "Rita" and other secrets too. Secrets were part of the culture. And, they were made to tell...over and over again and...to the next generation!

Santina figured she had been told a million secrets in her life and could be trusted with each of them. Perhaps the most important secret of her life was one involving her husband, Vito. He was a good man, who worked every day of his life and provided for his family. But he had a secret too.

Vito's mother Patrizia and father Dominick married at the ripe old age of sixteen. But just a few months after the wedding, his father was called into military service. Three months later the family was notified that he died during a naval maneuver. A year passed and his mother began a secret courtship with the town judge's son, Tommaso. There were two problems with the relationship. He was married and so was Vito's mother. It was a case of mistaken identity...Dominick was very much alive. Twenty months after the announcement of his death, he gingerly walked through center of town looking for his bride. He found her all right...with an unmistakable look of shock on her face. Luckily his mother and the judge's son had a falling out and were also fortunate that no one knew of their secret relationship. She jumped into the arms of her soldier husband and took up where they had left off. She didn't tell him that she was one month pregnant with Vito. She vowed to one day tell Dominick, but that day never came.

Vito never learned that he was the son of Tommaso until he discovered a letter in his mother's effects which were given to him upon her death. She apparently had not discarded some of the things lovers exchange and unwisely never destroy. A small locket with a picture of Vito was securely snapped closed and sealed in an envelope. It had been returned in the mail for lack of a correct address. It was addressed to *Tommaso Biaggi*. The letter was a full explanation of the affair and the pregnancy. The guilt she held through the years could not be effaced by giving her son, her married name.

Dominick went to his grave never knowing that the boy he called son, was indeed the child of a boyhood friend. But Vito knew and clutched the honor and security of the only name he had ever known. He was VITO FORTUNATO and from the day he learned the truth, he wore his name with all the more pride.

It was only after he began introducing himself as *Vito Fortunato... the loving son of Dominick Fortunato* that Santina questioned him and also learned the truth.

There was never a question as to what they should do with the information. Vito took it to his grave and Santina would do the same. The locket had been dismantled and all traces of the ancestry were forever destroyed.

However, there were things Santina loved to share with her children and grandchildren. Among her favorite stories was how she became a *seamstress*.

In 1923 Santina's father and mother were renting an apartment in their house to an old woman from the country of Latvia. She was a seamstress and they called upon her to make a dress for Nicola, Santina's cousin, who lived in Massachusetts. Since Santina was the same size, she would go up to the woman's apartment and sit and watch her work.

The young teen was fascinated with the way the woman took cloth, cut it into a pattern and sewed it. After observing her during the first evening, she went downstairs and announced to her parents that she would like to become a *seamstress*.

During the next few weeks the woman taught Santina the basics and finally allowed her to make the slip for the gown all by herself. At thirteen she was learning the skills that would be part of her life forever!

Ironically, Cousin Nicola broke up with the boy and the gown remained in a sealed bag until Santina walked down the isle at St. Mary's Church in Rosebank several years later.

It was another event that provided Santina with her first job at the Neuremberg's. Her father had painted their apartments, located on Ocean Parkway, and mentioned that his daughter was learning how to sew. While giving an estimate for another job, he tore his overcoat on a nail sticking out of a closet wall interior. The L shaped tear would necessitate more than sewing...the garment would need to be rewoven at the site of the tear. The Neurembergs offered to have the garment repaired, but he insisted that his daughter would reweave it. Several weeks later, when one of the brothers remarked that Vito had purchased a new coat, they were surprised to learn that the child had masterfully repaired it.

"You send your daughter down to our store when she graduates and we'll put her right to work," said the elder Neuremberg.

On July 5th she reported for work and began her few years of employment at the store. In those rooms she received her college degree in business, international trade and majored in human behavior. She was a fast learner and keen observer.

She learned about the business world by studying the ways Neuremberg Brothers interacted with their customers.

To the onlooker, their dealings were laughable. For instance, the industry was based on mass production and large orders. When a customer wanted five hundred scarves, they didn't sit and count their order when it was delivered. One might say the *business of business* was based on some level of trust. Knowing this the brothers would send four hundred and eighty pieces and charge for the five hundred. However, when they received an order, one of the girls would count every item...twice...and report any shortages. There were even times when one of the brothers sat and counted them again!

Measuring and fitting singular garments was also laughable. The shop had many people come in on a regular basis to be personally fitted for a coat, suit or dress by one of the brothers. Standing behind the customer and holding the coat that was supposed to be "fitted," was Julius. He would clutch the garment from the rear and announce, "*Look...it's a poifict fit!* The customer would argue and they would exchange words; but no matter how furious the contest, they still returned out of loyalty to the two scoundrels.

The industry was largely controlled by eastern Europeans living in the city and most of the money was controlled by them...as well as the little businesses where tens of thousands of people worked to keep up with the demand. And there were always demands!

When the United States entered the Second World War the shop began to produce uniforms and parachutes.

One night just before a shipment was to be sent out, Santina called the girls over and spoke quietly.

"Let's join hands...I want to pray for the men who will use these." The five girls bowed and Santina offered a simple prayer. When she said, "Amen," she looked up to see Carmella holding one in her hands and weeping. The others were tearful too!

"When will it end?" questioned Adeline.

"When it is time for it to end?" replied Josephina.

Josephina's brother Carmine had been drafted and the family had not heard from him in weeks. He had graduated from Aviation high school a year before and Uncle Sam stationed him at an airport where he worked as a mechanic. He most likely would have remained with tools in hand but for one night when he joined a pilot to test an airplane. Mid-air the engine stopped running and the pilot panicked. The kid grabbed the controls and brought the plane to safety. Within two weeks he was sent to flying school and was serving as a co-pilot and gunner.

Josephina's family didn't know that her brother was sitting in a luxury hotel in San Francisco, waiting for orders.

He was not permitted to contact anyone due the secrecy of his next mission. In his most recent letter, he sent a picture of Tyrone Power wearing a suit. He asked that his sister buy one or make one just like it for his return home party.

Early the next morning, after receiving the letter, she went to Orchard Street in Manhattan to buy the material and worked for nearly three weeks laying out the pattern, cutting and sewing during her spare time. Three months later, Carmine was declared "missing in action." His plane was never found. As for the suit? It lay neatly boxed under her bed.

The war finally ended for Josephina on the day she took the garment up the narrow stairs to a large cedar closet in the attic. That was five years after the war had been officially declared over.

Santina sat gazing at the mahogany coffin and thought how strange life can be for some individuals. The dead, Angelina Caruso had lived through wars, accidents, sickness and disease. She had triumphed over the perils of living in a world that at times could be no less than dangerous to one's health.

Yet, the beauty of life gave an individual the desire to live forever!

What other perils had Angelina gone through prior to coming to her end? Who knows the secret pain and struggle of the individual sitting next to you on a train or bus or even in one's family?

Santina thought that the most profound words an individual could say were, *if I only knew!* The sadness of the words showed how recluse some lives could be...private and protected.

Through the years she came across many, so called, *private* people. They were the kind that held their life under a mental blanket...never opening up to others. It was rare when they revealed themselves and let only a chosen few into their lives. It wasn't that they were keeping a secret or telling a lie. The privacy of the individual was to be preserved, lest they show their vulnerability and weakness.

Now older, Santina enjoyed these quiet days when she could reflect on the various events of her life...the events that were known to others and the private ones locked in her mind. She wondered if Angelina had time to reflect during the last hours or minutes. If old age gave you anything, it supplied the time...the quiet time for reflection and contemplation. It was evidence that you had a past and promise of a future.

Perhaps the most troubling thing to Santina, were people like Emmanuella Casale. Santina could remember a time when this neighbor smiled and made many gestures of kindness. But now, she was bitter...no...embittered by the events of her life and could not let go of her hatred for her first husband, who had betrayed the most sacred trust married people had between each other.

It was on a Saturday morning during Emmanuella's visit to her family in Sicily when Santina looked out of the second story bathroom window and saw the woman's husband embracing a stranger. The little window was opened at the bottom and she leaned down and tried to listen.

There, before her eyes was her neighbor, bare-chested and smiling. Santina could not believe her eyes as she heard the friendly conversation between lovers. LOVERS! How ridiculous she reasoned. A husband and wife were lovers...not strangers! The bond of marriage was to be the only sanctuary for lust and passion. He had broken the vows of his youth and Santina was angered. Slamming the window to its sill, she watched as the adulterers separated at the noise.

Santina could only think of the great injustice being done to Emmanuella. How could a man take another woman into his home... into his bed? What had his wife done or not done to deserve this embarrassment and betrayal? Should she tell her neighbor when she returned from over seas and what must her role be in the matter...if any?

Santina stood in the silence of her bathroom, perplexed and troubled. Perhaps she should tell the priest! She moved slowly back to her bedroom. Men were not perfect, she thought. They were fragile...no...stupid, at times. Yes, in these matters, many were just plain stupid, she concluded.

Emmanuella returned two weeks later and knew nothing of her husband's betrayal. But the night had a thousand eyes and Santina was not the only one who witnessed the transgression.

Mrs. Pappas, the "Greek lady" from across the street was also an eyewitness to the affair. One morning as Santina was cleaning her front porch window, she saw her leap across the street just after the husband left for work. She was greeted by Emmanuella and then disappeared in through the front door.

Santina counted the minutes...that slowly turned into several hours. It appears that the Greek woman had been watching the indiscretion for weeks and was able to fill in all of the details.

Months later, the couple was heard arguing and screaming from their house. Santina then learned that Emmanuella's husband and the woman had met on the bus going to work. Their familiarity grew into a full blown love affair.

"Love affair?" Santina whispered in anger to herself.

During the next few years Santina watched Emmanuella's emotions change her character. First, she was saddened and hurt, then anger filled her emotions. In the end her face reflected bitter lines where there was once a sweet countenance.

Her husband finally moved out and a divorce followed. The children, Santina reasoned, were ruined and would never be the same. It was the first divorce in the neighborhood, but as the years progressed she heard of several more couples splitting up. Santina Fortunato thought her family was the most important and precious thing in her life and she would honor her wedding vows no matter what happened.

When Vito finally passed on in 1972, Santina stood over his casket and squeezed her wedding ring to her finger...vowing once again to honor her wedding vow... *For better, for worse, for richer, for poor, in sickness and in health...in life and in death!* She knew no other way to interpret the words spoken so many years before in the witness of her family and church.

She also knew she would never remarry. Her decision to remain alone would not be based on trend or tradition...permission or legal reasoning. Vito would always be her husband and she thought it best to show her children the bonds of love between a man and a woman...*in life and in death.*

The Seamstress looked up to see her four girlfriends...her Seamstress Sisters. Yes, when five individuals spent so much time together in their youth and shared their intimate thoughts...they were more than friends...they were family. Santina thought of those intimate times together when one of the girls would announce their engagement, pregnancy...or the unthinkable!

Antoinette was the last to be married among the girls. She was nearly twenty nine when she announced that a man had come into her life and it looked *serious*. Serious meant that there were honorable intentions and a young woman's dreams were finally coming true.

The girls had assumed that at her age marriage might not be an option. It was in her middle teens that she experienced something that made her wary of men and their intentions. She carefully guarded the experience and shared it only years later when the girls went on vacation together at Lake George, New York. There, one evening, in the stillness of the night while sitting outside of their cabin, she told the girls about an incident that occurred when she was just seventeen years old.

Mario Anselmo was a border in her grandmother's house. He was considerably older and no one really knew where he had come from and no one dared ask. He was an abrupt man, hard and distant.

Seventeen year old Antoinette saw him sitting on the front porch of her grandmother's house one summer night when she was visiting.

"Come, sit...let's talk!" were the boarder's first words to the teenager.

Antoinette walked slowly up the steps and found her way to an old, white wicker chair. She knew it was wrong to be alone with a stranger, but he was a tenant and this reassured her someone had *screened* the man. If his weekly rental payment for his quarters was paid, then surely there was nothing to fear.

The conversation was cordial and she was fascinated with all of the things he said he had done in his life. His confidence and self-assurance were not the kind of features that she was used to in her own small and humble family. Her father and mother were servants...her mother to her father and her father to the city building department, where he served as a laborer.

Their life resembled that of generations before. You went to work, church and an occasional family get-together.

There were no exploits, exotic travel or notable accomplishments.

Antoinette looked out over the porch railing. She felt safe! The whole world was watching their conversation, so there could be no question as to the intention of the boarder. Over the next few weeks Antoinette enjoined herself to the man and spent more and more time talking and going for long walks up the local streets.

But one night the cordial stranger asked her to accompany him to the garage to get an important piece of paper in his car. She innocently followed and helped him open the large wooden bi-fold doors. A second later they passed into the darkness of the old, musty structure.

Once inside, he pushed her onto the damp and dirty cement floor. She began to scream and somehow freed herself and ran. A moment later she found herself in her grandmother's kitchen running to the knife drawer. Years later she thought how useless a four inch butter knife would have been against the brawny man.

The screams had awakened her grandmother and Antoinette shared what had happened.

"I kill him!" she announced.

But killing was not necessary because the man never returned to his room. Investigation of his suitcase revealed the necessary shaving equipment, under clothing, three shirts, a suit and something else. Tucked in the side pocket of the case was an article from a Philadelphia newspaper. It seems the *boarder* had *boarded* elsewhere...in a prison for armed robbery. He had served his time and the article announced his release and rehabilitation. Unfortunately, the rehabilitation had not included impulse control. And there was one other item to be catalogued. A handmade twenty-two-caliber gun fabricated from an automobile aerial was wrapped in a black sock and folded in an undershirt.

The man was never seen or heard from again, but the events of that night made Antoinette suspect of the intentions of men. He had not molested her, but the shame of being part of a thwarted rape made her feel that perhaps she had done something to induce his behaviors.

"What did you do to this man?" her mother angrily inquired.

"Nothing, mamma...nothing!" Antoinette responded in tears.

"A man does not do this without the girl..." her mother continued.

"Stop, mamma...I didn't do anything!" Antoinette cried out.

Years later she would reflect on that awful night and know that she had been pure in all her dealings with the man. And she understood her mother's ignorance as well.

As Antoinette related her story in the sanctuary of Lake George's open sky, the girls sat silent and watched as she released her secret and pain.

Santina was the first to speak after the confession silenced.

"You have nothing to be ashamed of for what happened...this was a bad man who wanted to hurt you."

Antoinette lowered her head and began to weep. Adeline walked over, touched her shoulder, then lowered herself to her knees and held her. Now everyone was crying.

"Hey, I have an idea. Let's play cards," Carmella suggested.

It was over! Antoinette had finally spoken about that terrible night in her life.

"I've kept it inside for years and I feel so free," she sighed as she spoke.

"We love you, *Toni*, very much," Santina whispered for the group.

"I'll deal," Josephina announced.

"You'll do nothing of the sort...every time you deal...you win!" Angelina snapped.

The night ended a few hours later when the girls grew tired and walked into the knotty pine cabins. Santina trailed the girls and put her arm on Antoinette's shoulder and whispered.

"Sleep, my sister!"

Antoinette lowered her head to Santina's shoulder, took a few steps then slowed and whispered.

"Thank you!"

If confession freed a person from such pain, then it had accomplished its purpose.

It was approximately a year and half later when Antoinette's father welcomed a countryman into his home. It had been twenty years since he had seen his childhood friend and little did he know that Pasquale Aquilino had married and supplied his village with future members for its workforce...seven...and all boys.

Antoinette's father, Gaetano, read the telegram and announced that his friend and *family* would be arriving in six days. The basement and attic were quickly mudded with fresh plaster to cover the holes and cracks, sanded and painted. The attached garage was made into a large bedroom for the boys and the family readied for the arrival of the eight-member family. Antoinette's entire family had rallied to prepare for their temporary guests.

"Paesano...paesano!" bellowed Gaetano...his wife waving at his side as the boat emptied its human cargo.

It is amazing how one can engage in a full conversation, wave and count at the same time. Coming off the boat plank was Pasquale's family. Santina counted as they disembarked: six...seven...eight...nine...ten!

"TEN?" Santina whispered anxiously.

"Shhhh!" chorused her father and mother.

Following a few steps behind was Pasquale's mother and father. After the families greeted each other, Pasquale turned to Gaetano, smiled and spoke.

"Papa...mamma, I couldn't leave them, ha!" he called out with an apologetic shrug of his shoulders.

"There is room for everyone," Gaetano replied.

The two families trudged along the receiving area and made their way to the small brick building where they would be screened for arrival and clearance. The intake procedures took a few hours and now they were on their way to a new home and life.

When the introductions were given, Antoinette reasoned that it would be impossible to remember all their names...that is, except one. She looked across the living room and eyed Pasquale's oldest boy...Giovanni. He smiled...she smiled...he smiled again and then everyone smiled! That was all that was necessary for their parents to know that their children would someday walk down the isle at a church. These Italians didn't complicate things!

During the next few weeks they spoke in their native tongue and shared their lives with each other. Young Pasquale had been married for sixteen months, but his wife died after a short and devastating illness. He thought he would never find another girl to marry, but gazing across the room, he knew Antoinette would some day be his wife.

Several months later they announced their intentions and the family gathered in the living room once again to make the *arrangement.* Six weeks later the family witnessed their union. Of course the reception was held at a Chinese Restaurant!

The sister seamstresses gathered at Antoinette's house and awaited the rented Cadillac Limousine. Little Carmella was her maid of honor and Santina's daughter Gabriella was her flower girl.

At the reception, Pasquale and Gaetano drank too much, danced too much and talked too much! But that is what happy fathers were supposed to do when they saw their children unite...bridging a friendship that started first with their grandfathers, fathers and now themselves.

The dowry was a massive three hundred and twenty-five dollars, a one-night stay in a Manhattan hotel and a week at a cabin in an old coal town called "Wiconisco, Pennsylvania" that was owned by Gaetano's friend. For the kids, it was the "end of the world," but provided the seclusion they needed during their first few days of marriage.

When the couple returned, they were given the attic until they could afford to rent an apartment. For Antoinette it was a fairytale wedding and years later they had six children to prove that it worked...and worked well. Weddings and communions made for some of the most wonderful memories. Funerals too, somehow had the magic of making their own journal entries. No matter what the event, there was always some kind of interesting news to ponder.

"Did you read the ADVANCE yesterday?" asked Adeline to the girls.

"Of course I read the paper...what did I miss?" answered Carmela.

"Did you see that Albina Mangullo's daughter got married to a Jew!" questioned Adeline.

"Shh! You don't say *Jew*...there may be some Jewish friends of Angelina here at the parlor," cautioned Josephina.

"Ok...a Jewish boy...did you see?" Adeline again questioned.

The girls now chorused that they had not seen the news.

"Albina must be going crazy with it. You know how she wanted her girls to marry Italian boys," Carmella added.

"As long as they love each other...that's the only thing that is important," answered Santina.

"You know Albina is going to make that baby Catholic. Watch... you'll see!" Carmella declared.

Santina looked across the funeral parlor to see her oldest son approaching. Frankie was an accountant and the father of three little girls. He was raising them alone...or at least with the help of the grandmothers. His wife had died after the last child was born. She passed suddenly, just after the doctors discovered a brain tumor.

"Hi Mom!" he called as he bent to kiss her.

The loving ritual continued as he leaned to kiss all of the girls.

They were secretly determined to find a nice girl for him, but he would jokingly respond... "But, I don't want a NICE girl!"

"Don't talk like that...I've got a nice girl for you...she's Polish, but she's like an Italian," offered Josephina.

"I don't like Kielbasa, Aunt Jo," he replied.

"She's American…I don't even know if she can cook, but she's a good girl," the Matchmaker replied.

"And how do you know she's a good girl?" questioned Adeline.

"I know, I know!"

"Eh!" Adeline replied.

"Listen, my girls are fine! Grace's mother lives upstairs and she takes care of them," Frankie replied confidently.

"She is such a good mother-in-law, God bless her!" said Adeline

Santina watched as her son kissed the girls again, walked to the casket, knelt to pray then waved good-bye to her.

She knew there was no feeling of helplessness and hurt greater then the loss of a child. She loved her daughter-in-law as her own and was there holding her hand along with her mother on the night she died. Frankie knelt by the bed and held his wife in his arms as she passed. He cried till daybreak, finally falling to sleep in his mother's arms.

He met Grace in the usual way…during his high school years. She was the daughter of Colegera and Benjamin Scalia. They owned a fish market on Bay Street in Stapleton. Frankie was their delivery boy and one day he met Grace and started talking to her.

Santina remembered seeing little Grace for the first time and telling her husband, "Watch….he's going to marry this one, someday!"

Who can know what lies ahead in the years yet come? Four years after they were married, she began to have severe headaches. Six months later they discovered she had cancer. Grace left behind three little girls, an adoring husband and many broken hearts.

Now he was on his own. His mother knew his loneliness and hoped that he would find someone. Somehow she knew, like herself, he would not remarry.

"So Adeline, are you going on the cruise with the Alter guild from St. Clare's?" asked Carmella.

"This time they want to go to Jamaica," answered Adeline.

"I went there with Aldo two years ago and all we saw was Melanzanas. If I want to see Melanzanas I can go to Jamaica on Long Island. They have them there by the thousands," offered Antoinette.

"Black, white, yellow…people are people! You think only Italians are good? I've lived long enough to know that sometimes our people embarrass us. You can't judge the people by their color. Some are good, some are bad. The skin doesn't tell their story," answered Santina.

Everyone conceded there were good and bad in all cultures. Santina knew about color and differences in people. When she was only eight years old, while playing with the neighbor boy by the rail road tracks, she caught her foot between two of the rails. The school girl found herself trapped and unable to free them.

She screamed and the neighbor boy ran for help. It was an abandoned track, so there was no danger of being seriously hurt, but her leg began to bleed and she lost a great deal of blood. A family…a black family was walking along the tracks and spotted her. The father looked at Santina and didn't say a word. With his massive hands he squeezed the rusted track, freed her then carried her to his car and onto St Vincent's Hospital. During the trip Santina lay in the arms of the man's wife. The woman looked down and clutched her trembling body and began to hum.

Santina felt a peace come over all of her body and she began to fall asleep. Fifteen minutes later she awoke to see the face of the man and woman standing above her with heads bowed and silently praying. Half sleeping, Santina closed her eyes and listened as the big man began to pray.

"Now Lord, this here is your child. She's just a baby and you've got plans for her. You got good plans and we need you to touch her body now. She's done nothing wrong and I ask in the name of Jesus that you heal her. Now…Lord…don't take too long, cause' she needs to get home to her mamma and papa."

Santina opened her eyes and saw a look she had never seen before. It was if they had just made a deal with God and He actually answered him.

A nurse came into the room and announced that the police were there to question her. Within a few minutes, Santina's mother and father arrived and stayed through the night with her.

"She lost a lot of blood and I don't know if you know it or not, but it is a very rare type," the nurse reported to her parents.

"Where did she get the blood from?" asked Santina's mother.

"Mr. Rawlings, the tall black man who brought her here was the donor. It was a miracle because we had no supply of this type and she did lose a considerable amount of blood," the nurse answered.

What if the strange family with a tall black father had not happened along that day? Might she have died? Any time Santina thought to judge by color or religion or creed, she remembered a lonely Saturday afternoon when a black family saved her life.

Carmine Calabrese found out where the Rawlings family lived and that next Christmas sent gifts and a turkey to their house. A few days later a letter came thanking them for their kindness. The card was signed by Mrs. Rawlings. A postscript indicated that *Mr. Rawlings went home for the holidays* and did not share in this year's feast.

Years later Santina visited the old neighborhood and found out where the Rawlings family lived. Eight blocks from where she grew up, nestled between a grocery and a drug store, was a small two family framed house where they lived. To her amazement, one of Rawling's daughters still lived in the house. Santina told the woman her story and she recalled her mother telling her about the little *white girl* that daddy saved. Santina reviewed the events following her accident and learned why Mr. Rawlings did not share in the Christmas dinner her father had sent.

"I still have the little note your mother sent to thank us. I found it again just the other day while going through some of my mother's things. In it she said your father went *home for the holidays*." My dad and mom were so disappointed that he didn't get to eat that big turkey they sent. Did he go home to his father and mother for the holiday?" asked Santina

"My mom had a funny way of putting things. A way...that... well...sometimes people didn't understand her. You see, we're Baptist in faith and when mom said he was *home for the holidays,* she meant he was in heaven. My father died of a heart attack a few weeks after he saved you," the daughter explained. Santina leaned over and hugged the woman.

As the Seamstress walked to her car that day her eyes were filled with quiet tears. She reasoned that Rawlings might have exerted too much energy himself the day he saved her. Perhaps he had given his life for her. She would never know until one day, she too, would finally *go home for the holidays.*

"Vinny and I went to *Disney World* in Florida with our grandchildren and had a wonderful time. Tell your group to go there! They'll love it!" Carmella offered.

"*Disney World*? What would fifty old people do in a place where people dress up in costumes and act like animals," Josephina complained.

"We went to Florida three years ago with our bridge club and Marcia Feingold threw up on me! That's the only thing I remember about Disney World!" announced Adeline.

Santina smiled at the comments and thought about her trips with Vito. They went everywhere together. She would wake up in the morning and announce, "We're going to Lake George," or "Get your things, we're taking a cruise!" Now she had no desire to go anywhere. She had done all the traveling one could do in a life-time, but without her husband Vito, it would be just another mountain, ocean, old building or lonely hotel room. It wasn't that her traveling days were over as much as it had moved on to another chapter...a chapter without Vito.

Several years after he died, Santina did agree to go on vacation with a group from her church, but it rained every day and she spent the whole time in a hotel lobby talking about the past. On the way home, Santina decided there were times to talk about what had been, but people spent too much time reminiscing and not enough time adjusting to the present and planning for the future.

That's where she must place her mind...in the present, not trapped in thoughts of the past.

She decided to spend her days with her family. That was important as they needed her to watch the babies, the pets or the house when they traveled.

"Did you hear about the priest at St. Catherine's Episcopal Church?" Josephina called to the group.

"No, Josephina, we didn't hear about the priest at St. Catherine's Episcopal Church...tell us what happened to the priest at St. Catherine's Episcopal Church!" Adeline replied sarcastically.

"Well, if you don't want to know, I won't tell you about the woman he ran off with last month," Josephina defiantly replied.

"Oh, tell us!" Carmella demanded.

"A young woman…with two children is gone…vanished!" Josephina started.

"You know they marry in the Episcopal Church. Well he was married and she was married and now they're together, somewhere…where nobody knows. What a world!" she summed.

"And why would you tell us about the Episcopal priest who ran off with a married woman with two children?" Carmella asked.

"Oh, it's not important…the woman just happens to be…," she paused and waited.

"Who?" they chorused.

"Only someone who would never expect to run off with an Episcopal priest, that's all," Josephina baited her listeners.

"Are you going to tell us or kill us?" demanded Adeline.

"Tessie Trambulla's daughter, Marie, that's who!" came the answer.

"Tessie's daughter? NO!" Carmella answered in disbelief.

"Yes, Tessie's oldest girl!" clarified Josephina.

"I always knew she was no good…the puttana!" called Adeline.

"And how do you know she's a puttana?" asked Santina.

"How do I know? Well, my son said…" Adeline began, then caught her words and stopped mid-sentence.

"So now your boy is an expert on puttanas! A very nice occupation for a married man with three girls and two boys," cited Santina.

"I only meant to say that he heard things about her, that's all," Adeline replied.

"You know all about this woman because your son has given you confidential information, he heard somewhere…from somebody, and now you feel obliged to speak in public. That's fine because not one of us is interested in knowing anything about her," Santina spoke in matter of fact tones.

"That's right!" Carmella agreed.

"Well!" Adeline breathed aloud.

It was Josephina who leaned over to her and whispered, "We'll talk later!"

So a priest ran off with a woman in his parish! What else is new, questioned Santina to herself. She had lived a life-time of surprises and these days, no news served to surprise her…nothing!

She would often find herself leaving the day as she lay in her bed singing, "*What a difference a day makes…twenty four little hours.*" Seamstress Fortunato had seen many a day come and go…days filled with problems and stress. She remembered her father telling her not to worry about the little things, because they had a way of working out; and through the years she would watch others walk away from their problems and somehow…they would work out. Santina had also come to learn that people had little control over their lives. She kept thinking about her neighbor, Mrs. Whittier, who attended the Gateway Church in Richmond Town. Her favorite expression was… trust *God for your life!* Perhaps she was right…living should be all about believing and putting your faith in the person who made you in the first place!

Her mother, Lucia was the worrier in the family. Everything was evaluated on her *worry scale*. The only problem was - everything in her life weighed the same. She engaged every dilemma with the same intensity. Santina remembered hearing her parents *go at it* in the kitchen.

"Lucia, you have the Cerullo curse!" her father, Carmine would complain, reminding his wife that like her mother she was one to worry about everything.

"You, Carmine…you are like your father, Aldino. Your poor mother had to do the worrying, the saving…the disciplining! If I didn't worry about the family…no one would," Santina's mother would fire back.

"What does the worry get you? It makes the problems go away? NO!" Carmine would fire back.

"Ehh!" Lucia would call out and shrug her shoulders.

Santina would listen to them bark at each other, but never thought any more of their verbal dueling. She figured it was the inevitable consequence of two people living together. She remembered one night after dinner, just after Papa had died, asking her mother about their relationship.

"Mamma, did you love Papa. I don't mean marriage love, I mean...Love, Love?"

"Whatta you meana...Love, Love?" her mother questioned.

"When you thought about marrying Papa, was he the man you always dreamed about or did you marry him because you wanted to get married and have children?" Santina clarified her question.

"I don't speak too much abouta these things," she began in her broken English then continued. "When I meet Carmine at my father's shop, I see a nice boy. He was notta like the pictures in the magazina. He was a gooda boy. He was notta, how you say, fake! He comma from a gooda family and my Papa say he will make a gooda husband and father. I don't know how he know...I justa listen and then I say, if you like him, I like him."

"Then?" Santina questioned.

"What more do I say? We go outta...we talka to the family and we getta married. It was no com...compilication," her mother explained.

"But...did you love him?" Santina pressed.

"You aska before, do I love you father?" her mother repeated in response to Santina's first question.

"Yes! I mean the kind of love that makes you want to marry him again if you could!" Santina stated with a juvenile-like look on her face and tone in her voice.

"You father was a wonderful man. He givva his life for his family anda for me," she sighed as she spoke.

"But did you marry him for love?" Santina again pressed for an answer.

"Santina, my child, let me tella you what a woman shoulda do whenna she is ready for marriage. Let me tell you about YOU! First, when we saw Vito, we know right away, he is a gooda boy. You father tell me on the nighta you getta married that he blessa you both and hope you have a gooda life. He was wrong? I dona tinga so!" she began.

"But mom...." Santina began, but was interrupted by her mother who didn't want to skip a word.

"A woman shoulda not get married for only love. Love comes witha the years...not all at once. There was a woman in my village that could always tell if a marriage would last. She would watch the boy and his mother and the girl with her father. How they treata the parents...that was the way she know if they were gooda for each other. I remember you father and how he love his mother and I know he would be a gooda man for me," she finished.

"But after all the years we used to wonder if you and Papa...well you know what I mean, if you..."Santina tried to ask.

"OH!!! You wanna to know if we make love?" the old woman finished.

"Yes!" Santina smiled as she spoke.

"We make love every day until just a few months before you father die. Do I love, love him? Santina, he was for me, my breath and my life," she finished. Santina never forgot that conversation. It shaped her life and her love for Vito.

Santina too, had her own way of assessing relationships. When her own daughter, Gabriella, came to her and told her she liked one of the neighborhood boys. Santina remembered reaching for something to write on in the kitchen and found a small brown paper bag. She opened the *junk* drawer and pulled out a knife-sharpened pencil.

"What's this all about, mom?" asked Marianna.

"First, we make a list of all the things you, Miss Gabriella Fortunato, will NEED in a man. Then we put down the things you WANT in a man. Okay?" she started.

Gabriella watched as her mother whisked the pencil across the bag and made a list of things she thought her daughter would need to have in a man. The list contained the following: "Loves his mother, loves his father, loves brothers and sister, is a hard worker, can work for a boss, saves his money, has a high school diploma, has a good job...AND goes to church!"

"Finished!" Santina smiled confidently as she spoke.

"Finished?" her daughter questioned.

"Yes! These are the things that will be the foundation of your marriage," Santina confidently spoke.

"But...what about love? What about happiness?" Gabriella questioned in disbelief, waiting for her mother to reply.

"My daughter, if what I feel for your father is love...AND IT IS, then what I felt twenty two years ago was not the same thing!"

"Isn't love the first thing you need for a marriage?" She innocently questioned.

"If a marriage is built on love, this is good. You must both love each other. There will come a time when your love will be tested. In the meantime, who will put pasta on the table? Who will save the money to buy a house? Who will support a family when the children come? Ah...the marriage must be built on these kinds of things. Maybe you go to the movies too much and learn the wrong things about marriage," Santina finished.

"Well what do you think about Bobby, Mrs. Fagione's son?"

"Elvira Fagione is a good woman. Her husband is dead now six years and she goes to church and takes her children. She stays to herself and smiles when she sees me. This is the mother of the boy. You see the mother...you see the son. Now...what do YOU think of Bobby Fagione?" asked Santina.

"He likes me!" her daughter replied.

"So does David Klocksberg, the butcher's son! I see the way he looks at my daughter." Santina smiled.

"I don't like him...he's a nerd, mom!" came the reply.

"And what is Signora Fagione's son?" Santina said, as if she were interrogating her daughter in a police line-up.

"He's...he's...well he's handsome and strong and...." She tried to finish.

"And you like him?" interrupted Santina.

"Yes, Mom...I'm crazy about him!" came the answer.

"You know if you marry Mr. Klocksberg's son, David, we'll always have fresh meat and cold cuts," Santina jokingly replied.

"Oh, mom!" Gabriella spoke as she reached for her mother and hugged her tight.

"Your father told me ten years ago, when you were a little girl, that someday you would marry Mrs. Fagione's boy and in these matters, your father is always right. That is one of the reasons why I married him. These are the kinds of things you look for in a man. The LOVE...LOVE will come," Santina said as she clutched her daughter and began to rock her lovingly.

"Maybe you should go upstate to the Concord Hotel. They always have good shows and the food…well the food is Kosher, but we can smuggle in loaves of Italian bread, butter cookies and pastries," offered Carmella.

"No, we went there three years ago. Like you said they don't make Italian food. Maybe we can make reservations for Villa Roma," thought Adeline out loud.

The Italians, the Jews, the Irish all had their favorite vacation spots. The main attraction was usually the food and the social climate. These were safe environments which everyone spoke the same language and played the same games late at night when the children went to sleep. But there were other reasons why each group kept to themselves…especially during vacation time.

To preserve their national identification, the Jews, Italians and Irish kept to themselves and isolated their children by keeping them in activities sponsored by their local churches. The Catholic Church sponsored weekly dances and they proved to be a successful tool that kept Catholic boys and Catholic girls together. Santina reasoned that more marriages were made in the lower basement church hall then anywhere else

When Donata Zollo's daughter, Maria started dating an Irish boy from down the street, all hell broke loose in their home. The two kids would sneak around to be with each other and lie in the process to hide their young love. When her father caught them in the back of the house, he took the liberty of beating up the boy. It solved the problem all right! They eloped six months later. Maria's sister, Madeline, married the boy's brother two years later and between them, they had eleven children. So much for separating the nationalities!

As the years passed, there were many such unions and Santina watched as her children moved from their Italian roots to marry the neighborhood boys who were Irish, Polish and German. They were good marriages too!

One consequence of the changing times had the kids moving out to Long Island, upstate and to Jersey. Big houses and wide open spaces entreated the young people to move from the little neighborhoods that dotted Brooklyn and Manhattan. Some moved further away.

When her son Johnny announced that he was moving with his family to Florida, Santina and Vito spent a sleepless night.

"And why do they move away, Santina, why!" argued Vito.

"Florida is nice, Vito. We can visit them," consoled Santina.

"Ah...they go to college, get married, have children and move away! I don't understand!" again argued Vito.

"It's good for them to be on their own, Vito. We have to let them go," Santina spoke kindly.

They never spoke about it much, but Vito kept his sorrow inside, where men are known to hide such things.

"Maybe your group should go to Pennsylvania!" offered Antoinette. "You can stay in a nice hotel in Philadelphia and see the sights,"

"What sights? Philadelphia is dirty and you can't go out at night!" responded Adeline.

"Ah! I know where you can go! Las Vegas! Frank Sinatra is there with Steve and Edie," Carmella announced.

"Las Vegas! That might be a good place," answered Adeline.

There were times when life was filled with more important decisions then where to go on vacation with a bunch of old people. Decisions about purchasing a house or car would dominate their conversation and concerns. There were also the times of crisis when the phones would never stop ringing.

When the girls reached their fifties, they would argue that their "parts" were wearing out. First, there were the hernias. Each had a least one. Then the gall bladder doctors got richer. By far the most serious situation came when Josephina told the girls that she had cancer of the breast.

She invited them all over for coffee and told them that the doctor said she would need to have her breast removed. She cried and the girls cried with her. These were the times when they needed each other...when their friendship was indispensable.

On the day of her operation, they all met in the lobby and held hands. Santina held Josephina's hands and prayed as the others stood close behind. Then she spoke quietly…words she had heard so many years before.

"Now Lord, this here is your child. She's just a baby and you've got plans for her. You have good plans and we need you to touch her body now. She hasn't done anything wrong and I ask in the name of Jesus that you heal her. Now…Lord…don't take too long because we need her."

Santina could not believe that she remembered the prayer Mr. Rawlings prayed so many years ago. Yes, she changed some of the words, but it was the same prayer. A strange look appeared on each of their faces because Catholics didn't say prayers like that; but Santina knew the power of that prayer and no one on earth could ever convince her that God didn't hear it! The Seamstress didn't think she needed anyone to go on her behalf to the All Mighty. If He heard the prayer of Mr. Rawlings…he surely would hear her prayer too.

The girls kissed and hugged - then a nurse escorted the patient into a small office. Later that day she was placed in intensive care due to complications. That night the girls all gathered outside of the room and discussed who should stay for the night. The decision was a simple one for these friends who had lived a lifetime together. They all stayed!

Santina set up the schedule for the girls and each volunteered to care for Josephina in her own house. While there was a strict schedule to assure that someone would be with her at all times, the girls would converge on the house from the early morning hours and stay until evening when the patient went to bed. Then they would argue as to who would stay through the night.

Six weeks later Josephina was fully recovered and treated the girls to Chinese food. As they sat around the table, Santina reached for Josephina's hand and squeezed it.   "Jo,   you   had   us worried. Stay healthy for us, okay darling?"

With tears squeezing through her smile, Josephina mouthed,

"I love you all, my sweet sisters."

It seemed strange to Santina that life begins so innocently and moves through paths and tunnels that slowly erode the sweet virtue of trusting youth. Here were the five girlfriends, sitting in a funeral parlor with a lifetime of troubles and trials behind them. Now was a season of peace and reflection. It was a return to the innocence that is experienced by the very young...of those who have not yet lived through the perils of health, war and personal tragedy. It was a time...with time!

Santina Fortunato was the stability of her friendships. She was the one who listened and after listening and waiting for silence, would listen some more...to the silence. She had reasoned that one's personal silence is what revealed the most.

She remembered the night her son Jimmy came home from his first job. The second child was supposed to be an individual...set apart from the first. And he was all that and more. He arrived home after working at the butcher shop, removed his shoes in the outer porch in the back of the house and walked silently through the kitchen and quickly engaged the steps leading to the second floor of the house.

He paused to send a faint smile to his mother, then continued on. An hour later, he returned to the kitchen in his pajamas. Santina moved from the living room and walked to the stove, where a hot meal lay simmering and waiting for him.

She might have inquired about his day, but she held her questions and watched as her son pushed his food around the plate.

"Mom, I lost my job," he began.

"You'll get another," Santina spoke quietly.

"I made a mistake," he continued.

"Well...we all make mistakes," she replied.

"It was my fault and I said I was sorry," he confessed.

"So...now you know that you are not perfect," she answered.

"Mom, he didn't even want to listen to my reason," he spoke anxiously.

"Jimmy, some people are not good listeners," Santina responded, moving to touch his shoulder.

"Don't you want to know what happened, mom?" he continued.

Santina stood quietly over her son and waited. There was no reason to respond. It was time to wait and listen.

A moment later the boy began to tell his story. He delivered an order to the wrong party and the butcher lost the account...a big account! A smile filled Santina's face as she continued to listen to her son's story. As he finished, he asked the obvious question.

"Mom, what should I do?"

"First, finish your food. Tomorrow, you go back to the butcher shop and explain what happened. If Mr. Brockfeld will let listen, good! If not...go down to Leon's Hardware and see if they are hiring," Santina replied, as she cleared the table.

Harry Brockfeld was a strong, burly Jew who had lived through the perils of the German onslaught in Poland.

He was crude and abrupt. Frankie, Santina's older son, had worked for the immigrant for three years before heading to college. Brockfeld immediately hired James when he turned sixteen. Brother Frankie had learned how to communicate with Brockfeld. In three years time, they had never had a conversation. James, on the other hand, enjoyed talking and when he tried to engage the elder Jew, he would be answered in abrupt terms that usually found him counting out potatoes to fill small burlap bags or sorting through the spotted tomatoes.

The next day, when James walked into the store, Brockfeld spoke in his commanding voice.

"Deliver those two bags to Mrs. Ginzberg. You are already twenty minutes late. I pay you for being late?"

James picked up the packages, walked to the rear of the store, loaded the fresh meats into the bicycle basket and exited the parking lot. Two years later, he picked up his last paycheck and walked to the front door to leave. As he did, the storeowner spoke in tones the delivery boy had never heard before.

"James, you're a good boy. I wish you well. Study hard and make your father proud. Here, take this to your mother!"

He walked to the counter and lifted the heavy bag filled with groceries, fruit and vegetables into his arms and spoke, "Thank you, Mr. Brockfeld."

Then next Saturday came and Joey Fortunato, son number three walked into the shop for the *changing of the guard.*

"Take this bag to Mrs. Kaplan. The address is on the bag. And come right back, I don't pay for sightseeing!" Brockfeld bellowed. The torch had been successfully passed once again!

Life for Santina was devoted, never-ending service to her family; cooking, cleaning, sewing and shopping. It made for a very orderly and rewarding life, despite what "Ladies Home Journal" protested.

Her make-up was simple...fresh powder and red lipstick. She had several pairs of earrings, a few necklaces and bracelets to match. Her perfume was *My Sin.* Whenever she saw little pieces of jewelry marked *clearance* in a store, she would buy and save them for gifts. Vito would tell her, "I haven't bought a gift for anybody in the family in thirty years... how do you do it?"

Santina guarded every penny and somehow managed to save some in the process. When her first daughter was ready to be married, Santina wrote a check out for the caterer.

"And where did you get this money?" Vito asked in a complaining manner.

"You give me money to go shopping; I save a dollar here and a dollar there. You give me money for school clothes; I save a dollar here and a dollar there. Some wives spend; I save!" she answered in matter of fact tones.

She saved all right...two thousand two hundred and fifty two dollars for the caterer and some to spare for a gift.

Her strength was felt by all who befriended her. One day, while riding the subway in New York, she saw a black woman holding a new born and fussing with two toddlers at the same time.

"I sure could use one of those," the woman voiced as she pointed to Santina's baby carriage.

Without missing a beat, Santina replied, "You have one now!" She lifted her baby girl into her arms and steered the carriage to the woman. With her own baby under one arm, she managed to place the two toddlers in the large seat where minutes before her little girl lay nestled safely under covers. Seconds later, she exited the train and disappeared into the crowds.

The train door opened, Santina moved to the door and not another word was spoken. As the train pulled away, Santina looked into the window to see the woman mouthing the words, *God bless you,* with tears streaming down her face.

That was Santina...always giving...ever sacrificing.

She had been given a carriage for each of her children during her *surprise baby showers*. She had three more in her attic and now one of the collection would be somewhere in a strange neighborhood carrying some beautiful children.

"Why do you bother with people? They're always taking your time from you," Vito would complain.

"I have to help!" Santina would explain.

"And what do these people do for you, eh?" he continued.

"I don't do things for myself. I do them because the people need me...they need advice or help. I see you do the same!" Santina answered.

Vito was a quiet man. He kept to himself and was jealous for the time others took from him when they occupied Santina with their problems. Santina was available to people...family, friends and even strangers. If she saw someone in need...something inside told her to get involved with her talent, time or resources. In spite of it all, she managed to raise her family...never cheating them for a moment. If the children needed something for school, she found a way to buy it or make it.

Santina looked up at Carmella's brow and saw her squinting.

"And where are your glasses?" she asked.

"I don't need them," Carmella argued.

"You don't need them! You are squinting so that your face looks like it will crack. What are you trying to see?" Santina asked.

"Vincenza Gallo just walked in with her fourth husband. Look at her with a mink and all that jewelry," barked Carmella

"Look at her! She looks like a gypsy!" added Adeline.

"Vincenza's husbands are her business...not yours. She catches these guys, marries them, buries them...and marries again," commented Angelina in matter-of-fact tones.

"You all sound like you are doing the evening news for channel eleven. Leave the woman alone," Santina spoke in firm tones.

"The poor woman should be with her grandchildren...not with men - going here and there," Adeline called out.

"And how do you know she is not with her grandchildren," Santina asked.

"I know! I know! This kind I know. They have to have a man in their life. God knows what goes on...."Adeline added.

"Stop right there! Yes, God knows and you shouldn't get involved. It is not your business to know what goes on with Vincenza," Santina reprimanded.

Adeline might have had reason to ridicule her neighbor because years before, she almost broke up her brother's marriage. No one ever knew for sure, but he was seen driving on Forest Ave with her in the passenger seat. For several weeks, he was spied again and again with her, but no one could ever pin them down with anything. Finally, Adeline called her brother on the phone and let him have it.

"What are you doing with this woman? She demanded.

"What are you talking about, Adeline? He answered.

"You know what I'm talking about. Vincenza is with you and you are with her...don't deny it," Adeline scolded.

"What I do is none of your business," he ordered

"That's what you think! You are not going to hurt Lisa. She is a good wife and a good mother. You keep it up and I'll be the one to kill you!" His sister replied in righteous anger.

Several hours passed and Adeline was still cautioning and threatening her brother. Finally, he broke down and began to cry on the phone to his sister.

"You're a good boy, Sonny...and I love you. Don't do this thing to your Lisa. You will regret it. I will call you tomorrow and we will talk more. Remember, you don't touch another woman now that you are married. Go to your Lisa...say nothing...just end this sinful thing you are doing," Adeline spoke in tender tones.

As far as she knew, Sonny's wife never knew about the indiscretion and Vincenza moved on to her next man.

"Like her mother, the p u t t a n a!" Adeline spelled.

"Stop it, Addy," cried Santina.

Santina understood that people could live their lives unblemished by indiscrete behavior. Then, one night, lost in their passions, they could falter and lose everything. However, she also reasoned that while most people could bury their transgressions on the surface, they sooner or later fell into seasons of depression. She was no psychologist, but she did outguess a few in her lifetime.

When Isabella Scala showed up at Santina's door, two years after she married a neighborhood boy, she listened to the depressed young lady's story. Her husband, Mickey, was drafted into the Army and she was left on the shore watching as his ship pull out to sea. The war bride confessed that her old boyfriend called a week later and she met him for coffee. It was a strong coffee…they wound up in a hotel that very night.

Santina listened to the story and something told her that the girl should confess to the priest and then to her husband. She had committed adultery of her own free will and knew she had done wrong.

When your man returns, you come to me for dinner. Vito will not mind and he will be here too.

Six months later Mickey returned home and sat in Santina's dining room enjoying a fine meal with his wife. Suddenly, Isabella began to cry and Santina moved behind her and held her shoulders.

"I can't keep it in any longer!" she cried out.

The small audience sat silent and Mickey turned to hold his crying wife.

"I'm sorry, Mickey!" she said through her tears.

"Sorry for what?" he asked.

"I went out on you while you were away," She continued to cry as she spoke.

The boy sat stunned and retrieved his hands from his wife's.

Vito rose and announced what had happened.

"While you were away, your wife went out with someone. She came and told us. I can tell you that she was sorry the moment it happened."

Over the next five hours, the couple cried, yelled, fought and finally seemed to go beyond their anger and emotions.

"Do you forgive your wife or don't you," Vito asked then continued. "If you don't, then this marriage is over. If you do… you move on and you both remain faithful from this moment on," Santina summed.

With his head bowed, Mickey spoke. "I love you Izzy, very much and I want to be with you."

The couple stood and hugged. It was over and as far as Santina knew, the couple never had a problem with the issue again. That night in bed, Vito spoke about the situation.

"I'm glad the boy forgave her. There is much temptation in the world and they will have many problems. But they must be ready to forgive. You are a good woman, Santina. I don't know if I ever told you, but I am so proud of you. I love you very much."

"Thank you, Vito!" Santina said as she clicked the bed light and let the darkness overtake their conversation and a most incredible evening.

But problems didn't always go away by just talking. The Seamstress knew that sometimes a wrong decision and its consequences would stalk the individual for the rest of their lives.

Through the years she and Vito welcomed many countrymen into their home. For the most part, their adjustment to the new world was predictable. There were the usual problems in communication, but these immigrants were hearty and determined. But when Cousin Bartimeo Cangianni arrived at Ellis Island, he encountered something that he hadn't bargained for and it nearly cost him his life.

Shortly after he arrived in the states, he served as an apprentice to an electrician and seemed to be on the road to a career and enough money to bring his family over from Sicily. He had arrived early for work and stood waiting for Mr. Fergione, the master electrician under whom he was serving. Fergione was late and the job boss insisted that Bartimeo start working. The novice walked to his tool box and gathered an assortment of tools. What he did not know, was that just after he left the job site the night before, the city turned on the electric for the nearly finished structure. He saw that a junction box needed to be added at a given point and reached for the raw, uncovered wires. He was instantly thrown nearly ten feet into the air and over an exposed ragged steel beam. It severed his leg at the ankle with the precision of a razor blade. He was raced to the hospital and placed on the critical list.

He remained on a cot in Santina's front porch for nearly eight months until his leg healed and he was fitted for a prosthetic foot. Then with the courage and tenacity of youth, he went back to learn his trade. Within ten years he managed to buy a building and open his own company and marry Carmella's daughter, Linda Ann. It was no surprise because during his stay on the porch, she would read to him each night and help him with his language. She obviously helped him with something else, because one night Carmella and Santina saw the two holding hands.

The next day plans were made for a wedding. The priest was notified, a deposit for the catering hall was mailed, the flowers were ordered and a limousine scheduled. Now the only thing Carmella had to do was notify the kids they were getting married. Linda Ann and Bartimeo were thrilled with mamma and papa's approval and a date was set!

This was the trend in the Italian community. For nearly two generations they stayed to themselves and few married out of the national bounds. It was the third generation that married the Irish, German and English. If America was a melting pot, the Italians fell into the blend. Other groups were able to marry within the culture; the Jews; the Chinese; the Russians. Perhaps it was the language, religion and strict culture that held these groups together. In the Italian community the assimilation happened and there was little the old people could do about it.

The change was a subtle and unwanted intrusion into the pure strains of their culture. For instance, an Italian would marry a Sicilian. This was tolerable because, in essence, both were "Southern Europeans." Then, the children married the Germans and Irish. Still there was the consolation that the word European was evident in the lineage. Finally, there was so much *intermarriage* among the various groups, that as long as one quarter could be identified as *Italian*...the perspective marriage mate...was ITALIAN! A quarter was good enough some seventy-five years after the first group of Italians arrived at Ellis Island.

To an Italian, being "Italian" meant several important things. First, you must be Catholic! This was extremely important because to the early immigrants, Catholic was synonymous with a unique brand of Italian. And while the Irish in America also practiced Catholicism, there was little connection between the two groups. Italians who practiced other faiths were shunned. If you were Italian...you had to be Catholic.

Santina felt that the public high school broke down most of the walls of difference between Italianisms and other ethnic group behaviors. The Jews, who became an ally of the Italians, were quick to latch on to the energy and intelligence the Italian immigrants brought from their highly cultured ancestry. Some of her best friends were Jewish girls who looked and acted much like the children who celebrated a second generation of citizenship. It was her classmate, Shelly Finkelstein, who came to her defense many times during her time as a student in Port Richmond High School. The Jews literally lined Port Richmond Avenue with their millinery, shoe and clothing shops. Shelly's father owned a haberdashery and she never forgot to send Santina's father a tie or handkerchief on his birthday.

The Jews found a kinship with the Italians, but never crossed the divide of their beliefs to embrace a people who worshipped Jesus Christ. After all, Jews felt Hitler was a Christian and as such, believed Christ was the religious force behind the war and the treatment of Jews. Understanding Christianity and its history, Santina knew Hitler was no more a Christian than the curb on the street. She understood their fear, but felt they had nothing to dread from true Christians who embraced a Christ of love...not hate.

But Shelly and Santina seemed to move beyond religion and family prejudices. In the solitude of their trust, they pushed aside the differences and embraced each other as students, women and friends. These bonds transcended everything. That is until the girls reached dating age and Santina thought Shelly's brother Aaron was *cute*. Santina innocently asked about her brother and what kind of girls he dated. Within a few days, the *bond* was gone and Shelly avoided Santina in such obvious fashion that she thought she had done something wrong or offended her. Finally, the wall of separation appeared. Even as a young girl, Santina had the maturity to understand and respect the separation of people and their cultures.

It was different with the first generation of immigrants. Her father and mother knew that there would be no bonds of friendship that could transcend the genuine prejudice each felt duty bound to embrace. The one difference between them and the generation of which Santina was a part, was the graciousness each had to keep their thoughts to themselves. Santina understood the need to remain a part of her culture and part of the greater world. But the years slowly eroded the walls. The Seamstress would sometimes joke with her children and tell them that if she was a teenager in today's world...she might have been known as Santina Finkelstein. Oh, how they would laugh!

Perhaps there was no greater testimony to the amalgamation of people then the site before her eyes. The funeral parlor was filled with people from every walk of life. The Irish, German, Polish and other groups sat in row after row conversing and reminiscing. How strange, Santina thought...there were so many people and so much prejudice in their little world. Yet for a few moments, in a small funeral parlor in South Beach, the petty and insignificant prejudices were put aside.

Santina noticed that the discriminate behavior of people usually lasted for a few generations. While the first immigrants fought to preserve the integrity of the past, two generations later, their offspring were consumed with only the present.

Fifty years later ethnicity had lost its roots because education and humanism were fast replacing formal religion. And there was a counter rebellion, you can be sure, headed by the older people in the community. They struggled to hold on to their customs and cultural practices. They wanted the old world.

Santina remembered the time when one of the old men visited a new Catholic Church in the neighborhood. The interior of the modern structure was built with wall plaques depicting the saints instead of the traditional larger, life-like statues

"Eh! Where are the statues? Where is St. Anthony?" cried out Saginario Genovese....his words echoing in the small, sheet-rocked facility. The old timers grew up in the mini cathedrals in Italy and Sicily. They were made of large stones, marble and the light of heaven filtered through stained glass windows that were centuries old. Even the church had adopted the many cultures which now sat in representative samples in the hardwood pews. The new buildings were stapled and glued with modern materials that refused to resemble the intricate detail of a hundred craftsmen, carving, engraving and painting.

The funeral parlor was ablaze with talking and even laughter. The *professional wailers* were long gone and today funerals were a time of meeting relatives you had not seen for months or even years. The procession to the casket was followed by a three row jaunt to the family of the deceased. Then you'd hear the apologies and the promises to meet again soon. But for the most part, the next funeral would provide the only opportunity to see each other again. Along with the various cultural representations, there were also the "types" that made up the flock of friends and family. There were people who used the opportunity to genuinely reacquaint themselves with others, while some sought out the Wall Street brokers in the family or lawyers. Nothing less than "professional consultations" were going on all over the room.

Interestingly, some funerals were the birthplace of family problems. Santina's Uncle Bruno Napolito came to the family by marriage to Vito's Aunt Augusta. He didn't let his marriage vows stand in the way of his philandering. At the funeral of Bruno's very own sister, he made contact with a woman who was in another room...paying her respects to the dead. Bruno was at the funeral parlor every hour it was open and then some. Where was he? He was paying his respects in the other room...carousing with the woman. It was Vito who heard love noises behind a closet door and opened it to find his Uncle in the arms of this stranger. Without thinking, he slammed the door closed and walked down the hall to his family, who were in mourning for Bruno's sister.

Vito related his story to Santina and she suggested he forget the matter because Bruno's behavior was no secret to his wife or anyone for that matter. But Vito had some other plans. He, being a "Rosebank Boy," called his lifelong friend, Little Nicky. Nicholas Torini was a cool, evasive sort who had the uncanny ability in relaying messages in such a fashion that they were never forgotten.

Little Nicky just happened to meet up with Bruno at a local bar. There, in the confines of the small gin mill, Nicky relayed a message to Bruno. The family could attest that he never *played around* again. So much for emissaries!

Aunt Augusta would never admit to her husband's infidelity and went through life, as some women do, in a state of denial. Like so many other women she could not face the embarrassment of her husband's sin. But one night, while visiting Santina, she broke

121

down and relayed all of the dirt concerning him. Santina just sat and listened. Yes, she was good at that and knew that sometimes people just needed the serenity of an impartial, yet loving friend who would not ask questions or offer answers. Little Nicky was able to do what she couldn't. She never found out what happened or why her husband's behavior changed so suddenly; but she was grateful for the change.

Aunt Augusta preceded him in death and those who knew him, said he remained to himself and was not known to have hooked up with any other women. Knowing that Vito was a *Rosebank Boy*, there is no doubt that he must have figured who sent the neighborhood's most famous scoundrel...*Little Nicky*. He must have figured out it was his nephew Vito. There was no question that he would never dare consider reprisal.

"Auntie, how are you?" came a voice to Santina's left.

"Ah, Marie! How are you my darling?" Santina replied.

A beautiful young woman rose from her seat and leaned to kiss her aunt. Santina's niece, Marie, was an exquisite specimen of feminine beauty. She stood five feet eight inches, with a frame that held all the flesh necessary for a successful modeling career. And successful she might have been except for the polio which crippled her movement. The nineteen fifties had not been kind to thousands of children strewn throughout the metropolitan area. Marie's body had not escaped the treacherous sickness that only months later, was halted by the Salk vaccine. For Marie, it was too late.

"How are you, my precious?" Santina asked.

"Auntie, I'm fine!" her niece answered.

Marie was not really Santina's niece. She came to the family in a most unusual way. In the late nineteen forties, Santina's brother, Mario was stationed in Italy before coming home at the end of the war. While in Italy, his troop came upon a farm and found eleven year old Marie sitting alone on the front steps of the small wood-framed house which was nearly totally destroyed. There she sat on a brick porch, two wooden walls and a few beams holding what was left of the house. She sat still and calm as the GIs made their entry into her yard.

"Where is your father? Mario questioned.

"He is in the village!" She replied in her native tongue.

But her father was not in the village. He had been killed earlier that day in a gasoline explosion. The death was not even war related. Come to find out, her mother had died just after she was born and lived alone with her father.

So there she sat, flanked by ten GIs and a house that would not stand the test of the next rainstorm. She was taken to an army hospital and arrangements were being made for a temporary home in a nearby village. Mario spent time visiting her at a small farm owned by a fine family with twelve children of their own.

"Hey kid, how would you like to come to America with me?" Mario asked.

Three months later he was released from the service, took a plane to Germany then returned as an American visitor. Miraculously, arrangements were made for Marie to visit America. Twenty years later, she was still visiting!

The little orphan lived with Santina and one year later, moved in with Mario and his new wife Amelia. One day, she came down with a fever that wouldn't go away. The family doctor arrived and announced she would have to go to a hospital for contagious diseases. She emerged four months later with a crippling handicap. To look at her, she was absolutely beautiful, but the moment she took a step, her entire body moved with a subtle limp.

"I'm engaged, auntie?" she announced.

"Who?" cried out Carmella, who was listening as the two conversed.

"Hi Aunt Mella!" she respectfully called and leaned again to kiss.

"Is he Italian?" Carmella asked.

"Well, not exactly!" Marie answered.

"What does *not exactly* mean?" called Adeline, who now entered the conversation.

"Not exactly means his mother is Italian and his father is Irish, right?" chimed Carmella.

"Well, not exactly!" answered Marie.

"If you'll all shut up for a minute and give her a chance to speak, she will tell us," offered Santina.

"Well...he's Chinese and Mandarin!" came Marie's answer.

"He's an orange?" Adeline called.

"No, he's Asian!" Marie corrected.

"And what does he do...own a Chinese restaurant?" questioned Carmella.

"Not exactly," Marie answered.

"Well?" questioned Adeline.

"He's a doctor!" Marie smiled.

"A doctor?" Carmella questioned.

"Oh, how beautiful!" Santina proudly spoke.

"He's doing his residency at Downstate and I met him at a party," Marie proudly announced.

The discussion went on for a few minutes and then Marie stood, kissed the girls and left the room. Such were the associations of people in this or any community. Lives converged in so many incredible ways. A little girl orphaned in a small, obscure Italian village, was now going to be the wife of an Asian physician. Polio did not shatter the dreams of a little damsel who found love and happiness a life-time away from the place of her birth. As for Dr. Li Woo Chang...ironically, he too was an orphan and was adopted just after the Korean War...by an Italian family in Boston.

Weddings, baptisms, graduations and funerals were all considered "family affairs." The young and the old all gathered to celebrate and to mourn. But there were other occasions that brought the family together...events that she wished had never happened. It was on a stormy night in November 1947 when she received a call...a call she would never forget.

On that night, Santina was busy at her mending and sitting in front of her Singer sewing machine.

"We're trying to reach the wife of Vito Fortunato...is she at home," a strange voice asked.

"This is his wife," Santina replied.

"Mrs. Fortunato, I'm Detective Marshall, NYPD. Your husband was involved in an accident on Canal Street and has been taken to hospital by ambulance," the voice continued.

Santina froze! Vito left for work in the morning to work on a storefront conversation on Baxter Street, just off Canal Street in

Manhattan. She remembered kissing him as he left from the cold porch door. Stepping over the vegetables and wine she had bought for Thanksgiving, she remembered telling him to be careful because the weather man on television said a snow storm was coming.

In the next few minutes she learned what had happened. She made a few phone calls and moments later, was joined by Vito's sister Pat and her husband Peter. The trio ventured out into the snowy night.

The Dodge pickup truck moved slowly up and down the streets and finally reached NYU Hospital. Vito was in surgery and a nurse came to give her an update. He had suffered broken ribs, a concussion, but more serious – they suspected that his spine had been injured. If so, he would never be able to walk again. Santina sat quietly...and prayed.

Within an hour, no less than fifteen members of the family gathered in the lobby. The Italian family was a tightly knit conglomerate of personalities...rich in culture and expression. There was crying, laughing, reminiscing and encouraging. In good times or bad, these tenacious and sturdy Southern Europeans clung to their survival instincts. Santina remembered the stories her father told when she was younger...stories about the adjustment he faced when he and his paesanos came to America.

In the early days, just after this first great generation of Sicilians and Italians touched the shores of America, they were met with such prejudice that they received few of the benefits other ethnic groups received. The Jews also suffered, but they created their own society, isolating themselves in little pockets around the country. They also dominated Hollywood, and while the Southern Europeans found menial jobs, the Jews were given social asylum on the sets of movies as technicians, musicians and extras and eventually as major stars. They found employment in the world of entertainment and dominated the various fields for over a half century. But the two groups had one thing in common...they clung to their people and culture.

On this cold and blistery evening, Vito's family huddled together and waited. One by one, they began to fall asleep, but not Santina. She saw Vito alive and vibrant...climbing ladders and hammering nails. He must live...for his family and for her.

"Mrs. Fortunato...Mrs. Fortunato," a nurse whispered in her ear. "Mrs. Fortunato...I don't want to wake up the others. Come!"

Santina rose and followed the nurse down the hall. She eyed the nurse's uniform and fleetingly remembered playing nurse when she was a child. She could see her mother, folding a table napkin and pinning it in some odd shape to resemble a nurse's cap. She walked slowly down the long corridor, waiting to stop and open a door to her Vito.

"It would be best if you said nothing and didn't wake him, Mrs. Fortunato," the nurse suggested.

Santina walked slowly into the room, pausing at the foot of the hospital bed. Vito's left leg was suspended and bandages covered most of his face. His right arm was in a cast and his ribs were tightly wrapped in surgical cloth. He looked like a mess, Santina thought. She slowly reached to touch his leg and closed her eyes for just a second, when a doctor interrupted her quiet.

"Are you Mrs. Fortunato," the doctor asked.

"Yes, Doctor," she replied.

"Mrs. Fortunato, your husband has sustained multiple fractures, a concussion and we suspect some damage to his lower spine. We're waiting for tests and also for Dr. Volpe, who is an expert with these kinds of injuries. We'll have a full report for you in a few hours. If you'd like to wait, perhaps you should get something to eat. Our cafeteria is on the second floor. He turned and exited the room, leaving Santina alone, but only for a few minutes. Slipping into the room was the entire Fortunato-Calabrese entourage. No one said a word, but each somehow managed to touch Santina's shoulder or hand. They gazed at Vito as he lay still on the bed.

It was Vito's cousin, Lisa Anne who made the suggestion that they all get something to eat. Lisa Anne was the last to leave the room, but before she did, turned to Vito and spoke.

"Listen you! I don't make you no more Zeppoles if you don't get out of that bed,"

Lisa Anne was the family baker...no she was the neighborhood baker. She was an excellent pastry-cook and Vito argued that she ate everything she baked and never gained a pound. A few minutes later the ensemble of nearly thirty, made their way to the elevators and entered the hospital cafeteria. After consuming an abundance of food and too much coffee, they sat waiting for someone to come and give a report on Vito. The next six hours passed and the group was joined by a dozen or more relatives and friends.

"Hey, I got an idea!" Jimmy Catrone, Santina's brother-in law, stood and announced to the crowd. "We gotta do this more often. I don't want to wait for an accident or funeral to get together. You know what I think? I think we need to put twenty-five dollars a month for each family in a piggy bank and every year we get together for a big bash."

In a few minutes, it was agreed that they would save each month for a big party – once a year. And so it started that next year and was still going strong each July 30th.

"I'm looking for Mrs. Fortunato," called a nurse as she entered the cafeteria and walked quietly to the large conspicuous group.

Santina rose and walked to the nurse. A minute later, she stood over Vito, who was able to make a small grimace with his mouth.

"Say nothing, my husband," Santina spoke.

"Hello, Mrs. Fortunato, I'm Dr. Volpe. Vito's spine has not sustained injury and I suspect we'll keep him until we can move him to rehabilitation for a few weeks, then you can have him back."

Santina nodded her head and thanked the doctor. Seconds later, she was alone again with her husband. She looked down to see him deep in his sleep and spoke with an air of reprimand and relief.

"You...you! Why did you do this to me? You scared ten years off my life and more. Now you get better and come home...the front porch radiator is leaking again!"

Family gatherings came for all kinds of reasons. Baptisms and confirmations were really a part of the religious culture and families would come together, eat...talk and promise to keep in touch. Then there were the classic football weddings which tangled dozens of guests around a long table filled with hero sandwiches, potato salad and pickles. These were the times when the family would emotionally cling to each other again...if only for a few hours. But Vito's accident indicated that while the family was vulnerable to illness, accident and injury, they could not escape a world that became more and more complicated as the years passed. The close of World War

II opened up a new world of convenience for these second generation Italians and with it, came accidents of all kinds and varieties. And the automobile was no longer an exception.

A few months later Vito returned home and once again found himself in the groove of family life. The next year was difficult and pressed Santina to the verge of discouragement and despondency. Every dollar had to be *stretched* and things were not allowed to wear out or break.

She remembered buying a whole chicken on Monday and cutting and preparing it in such a way that on Saturday night, they were still eating it. She would carefully cut and lay out pieces for a soup, cold sandwiches for lunch, stew and finally dice a few morsels to put with beans, onions and garlic for a topping on Vito's favorite meal...pasta fagioli. The children never knew the sacrifices she made during that year, but instinctively, she survived and the year passed.

Years later her children would ask, "Mamma, how did you do it?" Santina would answer, "You do what you have to do when you NEED to do it!"

Yes, you did whatever it would take to get through the rough times and Santina Fortunato was an expert. She was full time wife, mother, cook, gardener, cleaner, washer, ironer, window washer, housemaid and everything else a woman must do and be when she leads her family.

Now many years later, she sat next to her precious girlfriends for a few minutes at a funeral hall. The room grew strangely silent and for a moment, the noisy conversations, laughter and tears escaped and the Seamstress smiled inwardly. Yes, Vito was gone many years now, but she was alive, for whatever reason God had! He kept her beyond the years of her husband and many of her friends. How strange she thought ...amidst this noisy funeral crowd she had time for such reflection and memory. She was now seventy six years old, attending all the celebrations emanating from a large family and offspring too numerous to remember, Santina Fortunato was experiencing an inexplicable peace and a kind of happiness because anything that could or might happen...had already happened.

Part II

The funeral parlor was filled with all the regulars in Santina's small community...and each face reflecting a kind of change. Everyone seemed older and different. To Santina, the girls seemed to radiate a kind of ageless beauty and timeless stability and stood out from all the rest. The individuals in the funeral parlor room had survived the changes in American life. They had seen the world transform in such proportions that it was difficult to comprehend life in the forties or fifties, let alone the thirties.

The famous and of course, the infamous of the world had come and gone. New faces replaced old ones and the institutions were also changing rapidly. A new generation struggled to identify with someone or something that would hold their interest. Santina could have told them it was not to be found outside of a family. With all the changes, the girls seemed to be the only reference point of the past for their young families, who were a constant reflection of a world that was and now was no more.

There was little that they had not experienced...as friends and as individuals. If there was a sickness...one of them had at one time or another.

Santina looked at little Carmella and they exchanged mutual smiles. It was ten years earlier that the girls thought they would be losing her to cancer. It was during a checkup that Carmella's doctor examined her and concluded that she needed to see an oncologist because something just didn't look right. She made an appointment with a specialist and it was confirmed that she indeed had cancer. Things like cancer were not supposed to happen to any of them.

They had survived so much and perhaps thought that they were not vulnerable to this killer. First Josephina was diagnosed and now little Carmella was stricken with cancer in her left breast.

Santina remembered the night her little friend came and announced her *condition*. Like Josephina, the doctor said he must perform radical surgery. Cancer was an awful cheat and now it had targeted the girls once again. They wept and talked and wept and talked through the night. In the morning, they walked to church and prayed, then went to the diner for coffee. Three weeks later, Carmella went for surgery and had the cancer removed…along with her breast.

Santina and the girls waited with Vinny and her children during the surgery. Two hours passed slowly then Santina motioned to the frightened husband to join her for coffee in the hospital cafeteria.

"I'm thinking about that first date in the restaurant. Do you remember?" Santina asked as they walked down the narrow corridor.

"How can I forget? You girls put the whole thing together and I was only supposed to be acting. Some act!" Vinny replied

"You swept that little girl off her feet, you know." Santina smiled as she spoke and reached over to hug him.

"I think I loved her the moment I saw her face. She was like… like an angel."

"Earthly angels get old you know and things happen to them. Now you must do something again," Santina announced.

"What?" he asked.

Santina stopped and looked directly into Vinny's face and spoke tenderly, "Vincent, you must sweep your beautiful Carmella off her feet…just like you did the first time in the restaurant."

They walked quietly to the serving isle and Santina watched as a singular tear slipped down Vinny's ruddy cheek. Now an accountant and successful real estate broker, Carmella and Vinny lived comfortably in a beautiful home. Her life, right from the day she met Vinny, was that of a princess. After leaving the shop she never had to work again, but never lost her sense of who she was and the reality of where she had come from. She wore the label *Seamstress* with the same pride as the other four girls.

One memorable experience, she would joke about in later years, came when they joined the exclusive neighborhood organization on the *Hill* where their new colonial home nestled between two older mansions.

The young couple had moved up in the world when they purchased the new house and were beginning to see the *other society,* made up of Staten Island's more elite population. No matter how much they gained in the economics of the world, Vinny and Carmella remained secure and unpretentious. They moved through a haughty arrogant and challenging culture with a kind of quiet confidence…knowing precisely who they were. But, there were experiences that did test their ability to stay focused.

The first activity they participated in with their *new society friends* was a picnic. Carmella prepared all of the necessary food to feed her family and packed it neatly in a new ice chest.

She was in for a surprise when the car bounded up the narrow lane and they sited the other picnickers from the *Hill.* Dressed in the latest fashions and opening boxes of food, obviously prepared by restaurants or caterers, the crowd appeared to be out of a page of *Town and Country Magazine*…a periodical Carmella had seen in a doctor's office. She remembered flipping through the pages and knew her family was definitely not in *high society.* When they finally parked the car, the children jumped out and ran to the various activities and joined the other kids. They would have little problem fitting in as they were well mannered and beautifully dressed…Carmella always saw to that!

As Vinny opened the trunk, Carmella sighed.

"My husband, I don't think we belong here!" She whispered.

"Just stick with me kid…we'll be fine. Be yourself, they'll all love you…like I do," Vinny replied confidently.

The next four hours, twenty-three minutes and fifty nine seconds, as Carmella used to laughingly report each time she told her story, went by as slowly as four hours, twenty-three minutes and fifty nine seconds could go. There were cordial introductions and pleasant talk for the most part; but it wasn't a world of real friends, like the girls she had invested so much love in over the years. A half hour passed when out of the blue, a tall woman, about Carmella's age, descended

133

upon the couple as they were eating a piece of watermelon. She was dressed in a long white skirt, matching blouse, silk scarf and large hat. Rich and impeccable didn't begin to describe her. She threw her hand out to Vinny and introduced herself.

"I'm Mandy Rudkind...soo...ah...who are you and what kind of work do you actually do?"

Vinny smiled and answered.

"Hello, Mrs. Rudkind. Let me introduce myself...I'm Vincent Bruno and this is my lovely wife, Carmella. As for what we do...I own Metro Accounting and Marino Real Estate on Victory Boulevard,"

"Does Mr. Marino know you own his business?" came, the curt reply.

"Mr. Marino was my Uncle. He died six years ago," Vinny answered and added, "I am the sole proprietor of the institution now."

"Oh...so you do accounting and sell houses!" she commented sarcastically."

Vinny turned to his melon and began to munch at the rind. Carmella kept her head down, knowing exactly with whom she was dealing. She had met this kind before...pretentious, condescending and conceited.

"Do you work or are you a mommy...what do you do?" she asked Carmella.

"I'm the mother of five beautiful children and I am responsible for taking care of the most wonderful man who has ever lived," Carmella smiled.

The woman stood frozen and speechless. How could one so miserable respond to one deliriously happy with her life and station? Then with an air of bewilderment, she brushed her hair from her face and announced her escape.

"Oh, I see Jack and Marge Connelly...I'd better say hello to them or I'll never hear the end of it...bye," she finished.

This was another world for Carmella, who knew the joy and excitement of Sunday afternoons with a dozen people wrapped around her dining room table. That was her kind of happiness... serving and giving of her energies to those she loved.

The couple had experienced excellent health. But now, as the years moved onward, they began to yield to growing older and all the changes that come with it. For the most part, it had been sweet for them. That is up until now.

"Do you think she'll be okay," Vinny innocently asked Santina as they took their seats near the open window in the hospital cafeteria.

"As long as Carmella has the beautiful boy who married her, she will be fine...I promise," Santina answered.

"Thank you Sant," he said.

Through the years poor Santina had collected several versions of her name and some interesting titles. Santee, Sant, Sanso, Tina and Sa,Sa...as her grandchildren would call her, were but a few names; "THE Aunt," Mamma, "Santina, *the sewing machine*," started another list.

The small Italian community loved its names and designations. If you did something well, you were given a moniker. Aunt Josie, who was famous for her caponata, was tagged the *"Queen of Caponata."*

If a person of a different culture or heritage hooked up with a family member, a shingle somehow would be found or created to label the newcomer. For instance, when a fellow college student came home with Santina's oldest grandson, Michael, and announced he was an "American Indian, the choice was clear. The uncles immediately tagged him, *THE CHIEF!* The poor *foreigner,* as they called him, never knew what hit him. As the various European cultures were introduced to the family through marriages and life-long friendships, their real names disappeared and they would forever be known as, *The Greek, The Irishman* and *The German.* It was comical because some of the younger children never knew the real names of these familiar faces.

Every institution in Santina's community had representation from every part of the globe...the clubs, the churches and even government. Santina's graduation class resembled a mini United Nations, with dozens of countries represented as the kids crossed the podium to receive their diploma. But names changed when the girls got married or for other legitimate reasons. In the mid-twentieth century, it was not uncommon for entertainers and the like to slightly alter the spelling of their name. They did it for *professional* reasons, so they said.

When Frederico Balsamini changed his name to Fred Baller, Josephina cocked her head and argued, *"Yeah...Baller... Fred Baller? I'll give him, FRED BALLER. He's got the map of Italy on his face and he wants to be Fred Baller!"* Oh, how the girls would roar with laughter each time she went into her act about his name change.

"You can no changa you face," Aldo would add.

But others had to change their name...to survive!

One time Santina received a letter requesting a reference for a person named, John Cantor. She immediately questioned her alleged association and upon inquiry at the office from where the letter was sent, she learned the real identity of the party requesting the reference. It was Johnny Canucci, now known as *John Cantor.*

The story of the Canucci family began when Santina's father rented the basement apartment to them. The Calabrese house seemed to be an endless maze of rooms. During those early years her father Carmine, added extensions, separated rooms, created closets and put in new bathrooms. Eighty years after the purchase of the little wood-framed cottage, no one could remember the exact dimensions of original architectural layout. A growing family mandated renovations...and there were many over the years.

The family came from the Bronx and Mr. Canucci said he was seeking a nice place to raise the kids. The *kids,* for the most part, were already raised when they finally made an appearance at their door steps. Five new faces filled the little rooms created in the damp basement and all seemed to be safe and calm until the Fourth of July in 1931- three weeks after their arrival. On that night, along with the anticipated sound of fireworks, there were a series of robberies and even a shoot-out a few blocks from the house. Johnny Canucci was seen running from one of the stores and was brought in for questioning. He was released because his family provided a believable *alibi.* It was a lie because Vito was driving home from work and saw the entire episode. It was the Canucci boy...*Johnny,* who ran in front of his car in a panic that night with two radios under his arm.

Vito went to his father and told him what he had seen and within a few days, the apartment was empty. Johnny Canucci's name appeared a few more times in the paper during the next few years and was heard of no more.

Now he needed a reference...but for what reason? Santina showed Vito the letter and agreed not to respond.

"Faccia del maiale," Vito said angrily, calling the boy a pig.

A few days later, a law office called and inquired about the reference. They stated it was that it was needed for an appeal of a guilty verdict. Mr. Johnny Canucci, also known as "Cantor," had committed a felony crime and needed some *support* from the old neighborhood. He didn't get any and received seven to fifteen years in prison for his deed. Changing his name, as others Santina had known to do, could not disguise or change the spots of a mischievous boy.

Santina reasoned that names usually fit people. One of the boys in her graduation class was a giggly boy. He loved and was loved by everyone. His name...Peter Felice!

It was Santina who tagged him *Happy Peter*. Then there was Joan Disperazione...a girl who was always desperate and anxious. Somehow the names just fit the people and it never ceased to amaze Santina.

Unfortunately, Santina would go to her own grave never knowing the depth of her intelligence. Girls in an Italian home... were...girls – the apple of their father's eye. Boys were different. They were coddled by their mothers, who felt they could do no wrong - and disciplined by their fathers who thought they were up to no good. Further, mothers had a strong sense that their sons were the "christ-child" and no woman would ever be good enough for them. Santina fought this emotion as she raised her sons. She knew they were always looking for their next adventure...and in the case of her boys...the next adventure usually had something to do with girls. She understood the nature of youth and the impetuous, uncontrollable desire to seize every moment. She brought them up in a righteous fear...challenging them to see a bigger future...one that must be prepared for now...to ensure success later on. She tried to impress on them the reality that they could jeopardize their future plans with the activity of one evening...one compromise and she never let an opportunity go by that would demonstrate this point. When the *ADVANCE* reported a story where a professional man or woman lost their license because of some impropriety, she would review it with the boys.

"One night...one mistake...can cost you your future. Remember this, boys!" she would preach.

Sometimes, when they slipped up, she would say, *"It's not a matter of right or wrong...or good or bad. It's a matter of doing something smart or stupid!"* They understood her and the back-up, if necessary, supplied by an available kitchen utensil...the wooden spoon.

When it came to the discipline process in Italian homes, there was an uncanny resemblance in the tool and mode of correction. Santina learned that the wooden spoon was one of the basic tools used in the sacred responsibility of raising good kids. When the girls compared notes, they found that all of their mothers used the wooden spoon to stir the pot and other things!

As for her girls, she thought only to preserve their purity in a world that did everything to take it away. Purity and chastity were things they must have on their wedding day and to her knowledge, they did! Boys...well boys demanded more teaching and nurturing. They needed to be reminded that they had a place in the world...a place that called for an education and strong moral character. It was the same message for the girls as well, but they were more receptive and obliging.

One night she sat with her boys in the kitchen. It was raining and plans for a camping trip had been cancelled.

She decided to spend the time just listening to their conversation as they sat around the table. Perhaps there was no more intimate setting than the family kitchen, with a table filled with favorite foods.

It was nearly one o'clock when they decided to call it a night, leaving their mother to clean the table and wash some of the dishes. She insisted they go to bed and leave her to the chores. There, in the quiet of the evening, she reflected on all that was and was not said and felt a joy and satisfaction that she had done her best in raising her sons.

They were good boys and would make good husbands.

Santina admired her seamstress girlfriends and the way they handled their children. Through the years each of them shared their struggles and efforts to produce good Italians and good Catholics.

While there were no priests produced and no nuns, they felt the kids did alright for themselves and were faithful to their families and religion. It's not that they understood all the teachings of the church, but they were born Catholic and were determined to die a Catholic. And because of this, they continued with the same blind faith of their ancestors and made the weekly vigil to the church alter.

Vito insisted on the kids going to church, but never went himself. He told them that he was too busy or not dressed in time and somehow was able to skip church for all the years of his life. Even in death, he didn't call for a priest and came to his end with only Santina in the room. She placed a Bible in his hand and watched as he smiled and clutched it. Little did she know that the Bible was his lunch time reading and that he had read it through several times. Years before, Vito had hired an old Baptist minister to work part time and he entreated him to read the *Good Book* every day. Santina found the tattered edition in one of Vito's tool boxes. When she opened it in the margins were written, *good, true,* and *do!* Vito Fortunato was a good man and loved his family with the same passion he had been loved. He was crazy about his wife and family and lived for them!

He used to tease Santina and say that when they were old, the kids should wait for a snowstorm and let them walk out into it as the Eskimos allegedly did when it was determined they no longer served a useful purpose.

"I don't want to be a burden to my children. Let me go in peace without all the fanfare," he would joke around the Sunday dinner table. He did exactly that...when he passed a week after Easter in 1966.

That was a funeral Santina was not prepared for, even though her groom had been sick for several months. He spent a lifetime refusing even the simplest medication and took aspirin only a few times to reduce his fever during the last few weeks. Even that, Santina mixed in his juice.

Italians, like Vito, lived cautiously...moving slowly as they engaged the various cultures. Immigrants and first generation Italian-Americans did not want to be shut out from the rest of the society...even though they kept to themselves. They saw the need to be part of a bigger world and told their children to learn the graces and cultural expectations. So insistent they were in not being singled out as a separate culture, that by the third generation, few spoke the native tongue. *BE AMERICANNA*, they would challenge their children! Not all listened...but change was inevitable!

The media of the nineteen fifties and sixties, coupled with the Vietnam War, challenged the best intentions of Italian parents. They watched as their children crossed over from opera to rock n' roll, church liturgy to teen magazines and disciplined living to self gratification and experimentation. The period ushered in a new kind of thinking and helped to disenfranchise children from the authority of their parents and their Italian roots.

In spite of these changes, Vito and Santina did not brood for the past, but held their hopes high that each child would turn out okay.

Santina looked across the room and eyed Adeline's grandson Robert John. Actually, his name was Cosmo Roberto Giovanni Alaimo, but they called him R.J. He was enrolled in medical school and about to start his residency. Here was a special boy who somehow managed to overcome the hardship of partial deafness. During the summer, just before he was to be enrolled in kindergarten, he came down with a headache that would not go away. After running a high fever for three days, the doctor put him in St. Vincent's Hospital. There it was discovered he had lost his hearing ability in one ear and suffered partial loss in the other.

R. J. was a charming boy, good looking...with a crop of black hair that attracted every eligible female in the community. He kept company with several neighborhood girls during the teen years, but the obstacle of communication proved too much for them and he entered college, then medical school quite unattached.

"Auntie, how arwh you," he called from across the room. The garbled speech was still recognizable and most people who were around for any period of time, learned to understand him. Santina waited for him to get closer and rose to kiss her adopted grandson. Standing next to him was an attractive young woman.

"Auntie, diss ish Cawel, auntie!"

"I'm so pleased to meet you," Santina looked up as she spoke.

"We arwh engajjed," he announced.

The young woman smiled and said nothing. Santina asked, "How did you meet?" It was then that R. J. looked at his intended and signed the question. She signed back to him and Santina then found herself asking a series of questions about the girl's family and how they met. A few minutes later, they moved into the crowd and Adeline moved over to Santina and told her the story.

The two met while taking classes in college. They hit it off right from the start and became engaged almost immediately. She was studying to be a research biologist and the two were planning on moving to Connecticut, where her family lived. As Adeline rambled on, Santina's mind wandered in memory of the girls she knew who had dated him through the high school years. They had all given up a treasure because they were looking for perfection...in body, mainly. She smiled and refocused on Adeline's words...it was an inward smile, the kind you feel when you are happy for others!

"She's not Catholic, but I don't think they'll have children," Adeline finished with a resignation in her voice.

"What difference does her religion make...he's happy, she's happy. That's all that counts. They both had a limited selection, so God will understand," Carmella called across to Adeline. Santina agreed, but kept her joy and thoughts to herself. It was a good day for J. R. indeed!

"They'll be fine," Santina added.

"Fine...but only if a nosey grandmother will learn to keep her thoughts to herself," said Josephina, who finally joined the conversation. If there was one thing the girls insisted on giving to each other...it was their opinion. They always had *something* to say about...everything! Sometimes it did get them into a little trouble.

As with any group, there is and always will be a little rivalry from time to time. Their husbands served to moderate the friction, which wasn't too often. In the early years they all seemed to be pregnant at the same time and there was the usual comparison of children and their abilities. It came to a head one Christmas, when Adeline announced to Antoinette that her daughter, at age of 15 months could sing *Silent Night*. Antoinette's husband retorted by saying, "Well, our son Mario can *fart* the bass part to 'Ole Lang Sine.'" Never again did Adeline reference the abilities of any of her children.

There was one special characteristic which their friends and family admired. Early on they learned to forgive and forget quickly. It was something to mark their friendship for all the years they called each other 'sister'. After all these years there was not one negative issue that carried forth in any of their relationships. During that small capsule of time, when they worked for the Neuremberg Brothers, they learned how to fight the forces that came against them as individuals and as friends.

They never fought for their rights…but for what was right! Those years in Manhattan's lower eastside provided all the necessary experiences to learn how to battle for their families and themselves.

It was during their last few months at the shop, that a new supervisor was hired to oversee the operation as the brothers had opened another store in Hackensack, New Jersey. The supervisor turned out to be a crazy lady, as the girls described her, who lacked the personality and skills needed to lead a business where the workers were on an intimate basis with each other. For the most part, each worker knew what to do and how to do it. Even the Neuremberg Brothers knew to limit their input to accounting and sales. The first altercation came when she criticized one of Aldo's patterns.

"This is all wrong, can't you see? The cloth is crooked at the inseam…see?" she barked at Aldo.

"Mrs. Flannery, I cutta this pattern a hundreda times and Mr. Neurembergama no complain. You are exaperta ata cuttinga theesa patterns?" Aldo retorted.

"You'll do what I tell you to do…do you hear me?" came the angry response.

"I trolla you what I'ma do. I no putta the Neurembergama labela on these, okay….I putta your name," Aldo fired back.

"Just cut them this way," she demanded, then took the scissors from Aldo's hand, grabbed the material from his hands and began to cut the pattern. Aldo just stood and watched in silence. Within a few seconds, she threw the materials down and walked off in a huff.

Not content to leave the workers alone in their craft, she then targeted the girls. It was Friday of the second week when Flannery stood at the doorway of the office with their weekly checks. Adeline looked down at hers and a puzzled look came over her face. Something was wrong…she had been underpaid for her work. The girls were paid a weekly base and "per piece." Right from the beginning they learned to compute their own checks, knowing the Neurembergs were capable of *adjusting* their pay based on their own - *higher mathematics,* as Antoinette called it. Adeline figured and refigured her anticipated pay and noted there was, indeed, three dollars missing from the total. Just before closing, she walked into the office with check in hand and asked if she might speak to her about it.

"Yes, what is it…I don't make mistakes in my figuring," the supervisor defensively started.

"There seems to be a three dollar shortage in my check," Adeline stated.

"Oh, that three dollars! I inspected your goods and found a few not up to industry standards and I also saw that you broke four needles this week. I made the adjustment for these in your pay. Is there anything else?" She tried to explain.

"We don't pay for broken needles. Everyone breaks needles. As for my work, there was nothing wrong with my piece work," Adeline tried to explain.

"Nevertheless, it is my decision to charge you for your poor work and the needles. You'd better be happy I didn't charge you for coming in late on Tuesday," Flannery snapped, then put her head down and buried her head in some papers lying on the desk. Adeline walked out of the room and back to the girls, who were waiting to hear what happened. At five o'clock, they descended the narrow steps to the street and went into the candy store for some treats to eat on the way home. A few minutes later, Mrs. Flannery walked out of the store…locked the door and proceeded down the street. Her hands were full…two dresses, a blouse and a scarf or two lay nestled under her arms. Indeed her own check was accompanied with some perks for the week. On Monday, Adeline marched into the office, closed the door and spoke as bold as she ever had before.

"Good morning, Mrs. Flannery. I thought about my check on Friday and still feel it should be more,"

"Oh, you do?" Flannery fired back.

"Yes, and whether you adjust it or not at the end of this week, I am telling the brothers that you took some of the stock home on Friday," Adeline continued.

"You're fired," She called out.

"That's fine with me. I'm not working for a thief!" Adeline spoke, turned and stormed out of the office.

None of the girls were going to work for a thief and neither was Aldo, who was helping his new bride with her coat when Flannery walked into the working room.

"And just where do you think you are all going?" she demanded. Then, as if they had rehearsed it, the girls chorused, "HOME!"

Within a few minutes, Mrs. Flannery was left alone to *supervise* the walls and machines...unattended and silent. The Neuremberg Brothers were due back in two days and the girls awaited their fate.

Isadore called Santina and told her that they let the new supervisor go and begged her to get the girls to return to work.

"I'm sure I can get them back as long as you don't dock them for the day," Santina wisely offered.

"I have to dock you for the day...you weren't here!" he replied. In the distance Santina heard Julius counter his brother. "Get them back, you idiot...pay them, we've got no other choice."

Santina smiled as she heard the brothers argue, then was told to return with no loss of pay.

There were other supervisors through the years, but Flannery was their most memorable. Their favorite was Giselle, who was brought on board to keep the accounting in order. The only thing evident about her ability to use numbers, were her own! She was a perfect thirty-six, twenty-four, thirty-six and the love interest of Harry. Giselle was a friendly girl who roamed about the work and sales areas and went quite often to the office...when Julius needed to give dictation. She lasted three months when Harry's wife, Joyce, discovered her. Once again, the girls were treated to a performance that could not be topped...even on Broadway. Joyce made an unexpected visit to the store and found her man Harry giving "dictation." But there was a sense of fairness in the altercation that proved Joyce was all right in the minds of the girls. Upon entering the office, she told Giselle to get lost. What was heard from the small office during the next minute was unforgettable! Joyce spoke the entire time and Harry obviously listened. Isadore listened from the other side of the door and was even "referenced" during the oration.

"That no good brother of yours, WHO IS PROBABLY LISTENING OUTSIDE OF THIS DOOR AT THIS VERY MOMENT tried this and you know what happened to him. Now you have the gall to bring this woman into THIS STORE…into THIS OFFICE!" Harry froze and so did Isadore, who then scrambled away from the outer door when he heard Joyce's footsteps nearing it.

Oh, how the girls laughed each time they remembered the incident. From that point on, the boys never hired any extras to help around the store. As for the store in Hackensack, they put their nephew Ira there as head of the operation. During the week one of the brothers would go to check on him and see what was happening. What was happening is that Ira didn't know what he was doing and to complicate things, they couldn't get Aldo to work there on weekends! The brothers begged him…pleaded with him and offered more money, but he refused as often as they asked. He did make them an offer that would solve the problem.

"I gotta Nephehew in a Sicilia who comma here and help, but he needa the money to get onna the boat," Aldo suggested.

"I can't afford to…."Isadore started to object.

"Shut up, Isadore and arrange for passage," Harry shouted.

Several months later, Aldo's nephew Luigi sat contemplating his new job over a dish of spaghetti in Aldo's apartment. He was ready to go, but had limited experience cutting designing and cutting patterns. The fact of the matter was…he had none! Santina, who was sitting with Vito, broke into the conversation.

"Hey, I know what you can do! Aldo…you stay a few days work ahead of Luigi and at night, you can give him the patterns and teach him with your machine in the bedroom,"

It worked! Each night, Luigi would come home…receive his lesson and copy Aldo's pattern of the day. The brothers were never the wiser and Luigi worked for them until the day they left the Jersey store.

The Neuremberg family finally closed the stores in 1977. Actually, Isadore and Harry died several years before and it was their sons-in-law who took the store over in the late sixties. On one cold winter day, after seeing the oil bill for heating the archaic building, they literally abandoned it. The area had suffered deterioration and the building they owned was finally condemned due to deferred maintenance.

That was one of the trademarks of the family...they deferred any and all maintenance until someone from the building department arrived with a warrant!

Santina took a deep breath and sighed as she felt the presence of her girlfriends all around her in the dimly lit room in the funeral parlor. There, among so many people, she felt an up-lifting solitude that comes when a woman has a strong and healthy mind. She looked at her beautiful girlfriends and thought she'd regret having to leave them when the evening finally ended. Tomorrow morning the family would bury Angelina Caruso and she would fade from the neighborhood landscape and become only a memory. The procession would leave the funeral home, drive by her house and then proceed to the Moravian Cemetery on the hill in New Dorp. She would be buried with the Vanderbilt family and take her place amidst the thousands of those who too, were only a memory. If a person left their family nothing else but fine memories then this was good, she thought.

Santina figured that a person must go through life making memories...for themselves and others. That best memories come from those people you helped along the way. Yes, the giving memories outlasted the taking ones!

Looking ahead at the casket of her friend, her thoughts slowed. If she knew the exact day and time of her death, she might plan better and do more. But then a woman in her seventies was not expected to *do more*; they were to do less and be waited on. These should be the years of leisure, travel and playing. She knew Angelina had done none of these...but for all of her years stayed in service to her children and grandchildren. Santina reasoned that Angelina Caruso must have stayed on the Island for years at a time...leaving only for an occasional get-together with family or...a funeral in Brooklyn. Today she would leave the tiny isle and never return.

Sometimes in the stillness of the evening, Santina would think of the quiet nights she spent with her beloved Vito. She thought of the hours they sat alone, reminisced and planned. When he retired the years were supposed to be just like when they were young…with time to make love and be alone with each other. She remembered the feeling she had when Vito's strong hands enveloped her waist. Perhaps what she missed most was his touch. Yes, these years were supposed to be filled with the selfish intimacy of youth and sometimes she pined for his loss…so young and too soon.

She felt her marriage was ideal…with all the necessary feelings and emotions that the union of two people should bring. Often, in the midnight hours, she would look over and see Vito sleeping. Then she would gently lift the blanket to cover him. Oh how she wished she could cover him again this evening.

"Santina, Santina!" Carmella called, knowing her girlfriend was deep in thought.

"Oh, I was thinking," she said as if waking from a dream.

"I know you were thinking!" Carmella smiled as she spoke.

"Adeline is hungry and wants to go. It's eight twenty! Let's leave a few minutes before nine."

Santina looked up to see several people putting on their coats and getting ready to exit. Then she spied her neighbor, Elena Petrinni. She was standing next to her fourth husband, Gilio and smiled when she saw Santina looking at her. Elena worked at the shop for a few months, but got pregnant with her first child and morning sickness caused her to quit before she even got started. Perhaps if she was able to work a few years, then she too would have been a part of the group. Husband number one left six months after they were married and number two emerged and tied the knot in less than a year. He absented himself from the house one night and never returned. No one ever knew what became of him, except he worked down on the docks in Brooklyn. In those days, it was explanation enough for anyone who left a house one night and never returned. Husband three was a career soldier who made it a career of sweeping women off their feet…Elena included. Now here was number four. Gilio was a good man who at one time worked as a carpenter with Vito. He was the first stable man to come into her life and he really loved her. The question remained…did Elena love him. After four husbands, one might begin to suspect whether there was enough love or energy in anyone to trust, honor and obey!

Elena still lived in the house where she was born and never worked other than the time put in at Neuremberg's. Her parents, who lived on the top floor managed to pay her way through life, then left a large inheritance when they died...including the house, country cabin and some stocks. Santina wondered if Elena was happy with her life...the way she was with hers. She would never know for sure because Elena spent her life smiling...at anything and anyone... especially men. It must have been easy to go through life without a care, but then how could one see the hurt, shame or disappointment inside...deep inside of an individual. Santina never let herself think she knew the intimate feelings of those around her...let alone Elena Petrinni.

Santina glanced at the casket and wondered if the same crowd would show up for her *festivities*. She wondered what they would say and who would say it. Her son's-in-law surely would speak...as well as her children on that fateful day.

"Santina Fortunato! Come stai?" a voice asked. People speaking the old language with its dialects these days were certainly the old-timers and an old-timer it was indeed. Signora Verilli was another person with whom Santina could attach the early years. She somehow outlived her husband and three sons. She was a sturdy sort, with all the strength one could find in a forty year old woman and at eighty-five she was still beautiful and stately.

Pina Verilli was a remnant of the past...a living memory for those who knew the early days and remembered them with a smile. Her husband, Greco, was an auto mechanic who had died just eight months before. Through the years he had repaired most of the cars in the neighborhood...with no charge. They were good people...determined to make it in America and help others *make it* too!

They had come off the boat from Italy with a few dollars in their pocket. Upon arrival, he had contracted, what they thought was, conjunctivitis in his right eye and they were immediately scheduled for deportation when a miracle occurred. Left alone by the intake officers in a small, damp waiting room, Pina grabbed her husband's hand and brought it up with hers to his swollen eye.

"God...you taka this away! You bring us here...now you no let them taka us backa to Sicilia!" She cried out as if giving an order.

Greco went to the men's room, washed his face and came out five minutes later. The swelling was gone and his vision had returned.

"I'm fine, Signora! And you?" Santina called to her.

"Summa days are good...eh, summa bad. I missa my husband," She answered like so many of her peers.

So often this was the reply from the old people. Of course some days were good and bad, but the woman was alive and could testify to the passing days...one at a time and this made all days "good."

Santina looked at the clock on the wall and her eyes fell south-ward to the two men standing next to each other. Frank Trattore and Sal Visconti were the adopted sons of the neighborhood. They owned the oil company that provided the fuel for heating their houses. First owned by their fathers, the two boys had gone to college and sought out career options other than the hard work of the heating oil busi-ness. When their fathers were no longer able to run business, the College grads looked at the books and couldn't believe how much money the business generated. They made up their minds to carry on the business and, like their fathers, Frank and Sal occasionally drove the big oil trucks - stopping in to chat with each customer. Santina remembered the generosity of their fathers during the tough depres-sion years. It was not uncommon for the men to wait for payment and in some cases, payment never came. Still they delivered the precious oil to all of their customers.

Leno and Sal Sr. started the business in the twenties after purchasing a broken down Brockway truck and a few dozen accounts from Adolph Deutch for three hundred dollars. Deutch, a German who came to the country in the 1870s, became too old to carry on and the two paesanos took a gamble...a gamble that paid off. These days, nearly a dozen trucks still carried number two crude oil to hundreds of homes. It was nice to see the sons still working together like their father did so many years before.

Frank walked over to Santina and kissed her on the cheek. Such was the custom in the Italian community. It was called *respect*!

"Mrs. Fortunato, how are you doing?" Frank asked.

"I am fine...and you and your lovely family?" she asked in reply.

"Connie is pregnant with our third," he answered.

"Come by my house next time you are in the neighborhood...I have something for when the baby come," Santina said.

"You don't have to...." Frank began, but was interrupted.

"I don't have to do what I do. I am the adopted aunt, so you don't tell me I don't have to...All right!" Santina rambled and reached up to kiss her oilman.

"Thank you," He respectfully replied.

"I thank you boys and your father and uncle for the concern and love they showed us when times were tough for my parents. You don't know those days, but I do...and I will never forget them."

Santina watched as the strapping young man made his way back to his partner, who now seeing Santina, threw a kiss to her.

"Good boys, they are," she whispered to Carmella who leaned over to tell her something. She quickly returned to her quiet thoughts. It always fascinated Santina how the old folks managed on the little income they made over the years. Her parents never made much more than the minimum wage, but managed to leave each of their children nearly ten thousand dollars and a house, that had been paid off years before. Perhaps no parents sacrificed more than Josephina's. Her father worked in a grocery store as a stocker and clerk and her mother was a seamstress. Through the years, Josephina could never get them to buy a car or new clothes. They lived modestly, to say the least, and she never imagined they would leave any kind of inheritance. Yet, at their death they left nearly seventy thousand dollars.

Upon investigation, she found out that her father first thought he had been "swindled" by a few neighbors into buying some stock. He told his wife he had bought some stock and didn't know whether to sell it or buy some more. He was advised by Mr. Goldman, the man who did his yearly taxes, to continue to buy the stock...that it was a good long term investment. He never spoke of any dividends and Josephina even used her own money to bury him. A year later her mother died. Several months after she passed on, Josephina found a bundle of stocks indeed. They were tucked in a large envelope in a desk drawer in the upstairs hallway. She stood in amazement as she read the front cover of a large envelope holding the stocks neatly tied in string. It read...*American Telephone & Telegraph*. He had bought the stocks, one at a time and made partial payment for each until it was paid in full. Her father had accumulated over twenty years of stock issues...one every couple of months.

None of the girls expected any money when their parents died. Having never made any great amount of money from the simple jobs each had, their careful savings and conservation through the years would now benefit their children and grandchildren. This was their dream and hope for the future of their respective families. Interestingly, the parents of the girls only met a few times over the years and remained relative strangers. Not their daughters! They would share intimacies, struggles and triumphs that would shape their relationships and their love for each other.

The seamstress quintet thought differently about inheritance. They wanted to leave a legacy and didn't want to make a mistake as to what kind it should be. They had learned lessons by observing other parents and were determined to leave something in addition to money!

Manny and Ulanda Pirandello worked all of their lives and saved every penny they could so that their children might have money to buy a house and the finer things in life. Manny was a maintenance worker at the local post office and Ulanda worked in a bakery. These Italian immigrants saw the struggle of their countrymen and were determined to rise above the poverty they had known in Italy.

Up at 4:00 a.m. each morning, Ulanda rushed to make breakfast, pack lunches and even set the evening meal menu in place. Then, at 4:45 a.m. she boarded a bus, the Staten Island Ferry, a subway and then walked for twenty minutes to get to the bakery owned by her brother and his partner. In the early evening hours, she would retrace her morning hike to get back home and prepare for her evening housework. This was her life...seven days a week! Her children were well cared for by her mother and their needs were met. But something must have been missing because in their mid teen years they rebelled...and oh, did they rebel.

Benny was hauled to the police station for smoking marijuana and drinking and Christine knew all the boys in the neighborhood...

personally. The couple had lost their children while trying to prepare for the future. For the sake of a paycheck, they were hardly ever home.

When the children were in their early twenties, both parents and the grandmother died in a period of eighteen months leaving the family "fortune" to the children. The Seamstresses watched as the money disappeared in a matter of months. In the end, the couple had given their children all of the money needed to attend the college of their choice and the resources to secure a future in a profession, but they had not provided the most important thing of all…their presence and daily wisdom. Benny spent his life in aimless pursuit of something he could not find and Christine went from man to man…then husband to husband in search of something they could not give.

The girls never forgot what they witnessed and vowed to provide their children with the love and guidance Manny and Ulanda had failed to offer their two children. They had invested their time elsewhere…where there were no lasting dividends.

One of the biggest struggles the girls had was convincing some of their children to go to college. They wanted their children to succeed and mapped out a *success plan* for each. Guido, Antoinette's youngest boy dropped out after one semester and decided to go to work at a local auto garage. Antoinette fought with him for months about not completing his college education.

"But mom, this is what I want to do. College is not for me," he pleaded.

"I don't want you to work at a garage. I want more than just a job," Antoinette challenged him.

"More…More? What's this thing with "more?" I can make a good living in the garage and someday own my own shop. Andy, my boss, says I've got talent. Mom…he says I've got talent. Please trust me. I won't disappoint you," he pledged.

"I don't know what I'm going to do with Guido. He wants to be a mechanic," Antoinette told Santina one night over coffee.

"Leave him alone, Antoinette. He'll be fine. Give him some time to think and work it out for himself," Santina told her wisely.

It did work out! Eight years later he opened his own service station on Amboy Road.

The funeral director walked to the front of the room and addressed the group. Santina moved from her conversations and focused on his words.

"The family has requested that if anyone has anything they would like to say about their mother, please come up and share it. Perhaps you have a memory you would like to tell us about."

Santina's eyes scanned the room and watched as Pasquale Calzaranno moved slowly to the casket area. He had no other choice but to move slowly as he weighed an easy four-hundred pounds.

"I met Mrs. Caruso nearly twenty-five years ago when I delivered groceries to her house," he began, but was interrupted by his own tears. "She was like a mother to me and I especially remember her generosity when I needed new sneakers. She gave me a job cleaning out her basement and painting her back door. I earned just enough to buy a new pair of Keds," he finished.

He walked from the front of the room in tears and was greeted and helped by his brother Sal, who also loved pasta!

Frances Martini took the spotlight and told how Angelina gave clothing for her baby when her husband was sent overseas. Bella Notobene shared her story of their meeting at a train station one wet January night. She slipped on some ice and fell on the hard concrete station floor. It was Angelina who held her and stayed until her husband came to get her.

For the next fifteen minutes various people made their way to the front and shared their stories. The family was beaming... but drenched in tears as the stories unfolded. Finally Angelina's youngest daughter, Jenny, stepped up to thank the people for coming and announced where the burial would take place the next morning and at what restaurant they would meet afterward.

Santina admired her poise and grace. Little Jenny, Angelina's youngest was a lawyer and doing well at her firm. But *Little Jenny*, so tagged because Angelina's sister-in-law was big Jenny, gave quite a bit of trouble in her teen years. At thirteen she started smoking, then drinking. When her father decided he had enough, he took matters into his own hands.

He waited up one night until his errant daughter came home from the movies. In the solitude of their living room, he took off his belt and strapped her five times. He was calm and administered the punishment in quick rapid strokes. The energy exerted in the matter did not amount to much as he wanted the lesson to be learned by stripping a bit of dignity and pride rather then hurting her.

"The next time you disobey me or your mother, you will pack your bags and leave. Do you understand?" he announced in his firmest voice. From that point on, she never again challenged their authority.

Santina and Vito never took a strap to their children. It was never necessary! Santina did administer the *wooden spoon* on many occasions when the children needed correction...but she never struck them in anger. Vito would give his children one of his looks and they would melt into tears. There was order their home because Santina yielded to Vito's authority. In doing so, the children also yielded. There was a clear definition of leadership in the house and it was understood that everyone answered to papa.

The night was slowly coming to a close and Santina watched as two people walked into the room from the side door. The night darkness crept in behind them.

"What are they doing here?" called Antoinette.

"Everyone and anyone can come to a funeral," Adeline answered.

"Not when people have done what they've done!" Antoinette countered.

At one time, Thomas and Beverly Pinto, cousins by marriage, were tenants in Angelina's upper apartment. They left owing six months rent and trashed the apartment before leaving. No one had seen them in years because they had moved to Toronto, Canada. It cost thousands of dollars to restore the apartment and left Angelina in quite a bit of debt. Her husband vowed to get them for what they had done but he never could locate them.

As they proceeded to the casket, two of Angelina's sons rose to meet the couple. The girls watched as the families converged in front of the flower arrangement. Words were exchanged and, to everyone's surprise, the family members moved aside and let the couple pay their last respects. Nothing more was said and they exited the room a few minutes later without incident.

Perhaps that was best, reasoned Santina as she studied the five minute event. Grudges trapped people and held them in time... in fear and anger. The whole world should forgive like this, she thought, but that was easier said then done for most. She too, had to learn how to forgive and reasoned that one does not forget...it is a necessary function of the mind and cannot be shielded from the memory. She once read that forgiveness was the willful emptying of oneself and taking on the very character of God. She learned to live by that code.

Several years after she was married, Santina learned that a woman, for whom Vito was working, hoped for more than fresh paint on her living room walls. One morning, when he reported for work, he found the furniture draped in sheets and the homeowner draped only in the morning light, which enveloped her while lying on the couch. Vito turned, took his supplies and left the house. At home, he told his wife about the incident. Perhaps it might have been forgivable, but it was one of Santina's best friends in high school. Anger and hatred secretly festered for months until she reasoned these feelings were not accomplishing anything. She went to the priest and asked for help and he told her to forgive the woman and not hold to these destructive emotions. That is not what she wanted to hear. She confided in the girls and received a variety of "remedies" ranging from confrontation to anonymous letter writing. There was no peace until Santina confronted herself one night when a fit of anger seemed to possess her. She pleaded with God to help her and the feelings were gone...almost instantly.

Those were the younger days...when life would overwhelm her with duties of marriage and motherhood. Raising children was the biggest challenge she had ever faced. It encompassed all of her time and energy and provided few moments for self-indulgence and destructive emotions. If a person can discover anything in life...they must learn how to forgive others and themselves. Santina learned she could manage these emotions, while other pressures of life eluded her. One, was the how to use her time!

The passage of time was something she could not control. Santina attempted to redeem the minutes...days and years, but somehow time challenged her and she found herself always struggling to do the things she needed and wanted to do. The luxury of time evaded the Seamstress and left her weary in the late evenings when she collapsed in her bed next to Vito.

It was on one of these nights that Santina turned to Vito and spoke about their struggles.

"Vito, you and I are tired...too tired to live as we should."

"And how should we live? What do you want from me? We work...we eat...we raise our children. This is what we must do. There is nothing else," he replied.

"There has to be more, my husband," Santina spoke passionately.

"I don't think so, Santina," Vito replied.

"It is not for myself, that I want...but for you and me...something for us," she spoke again in such passion that Vito sat up.

"Santina, come to me," he reached for her as he spoke tenderly to comfort and reassure her.

The two held each other and kissed. No one would know that they loved every day of their marriage and only when they were apart did they deny each other the intimacy of their union.

Sometimes, when the night was still, Santina would think of the days before the children came along and recall the times she spent at Midland and South Beach. Amidst the cascading waves, she would look over to New Jersey and think perhaps they should move there. But Staten Island had become home. It was private and distant from the crowds in the other boroughs and the busy shore communities of its sister state. The ferry ride across to Brooklyn produced enough separation from the other boroughs and provided the seclusion she felt her family needed. Staten Islanders were different. Many residents were Italian...some Irish and others German. It was strewn with trees, grass and dirt. Pebble-stone roads still cut through woodlands and the few old and new neighborhoods. For Santina this was home and always would be for her family.

Dotted throughout the north and south shore were little communities of Sicilians and Italians. They converged on the Island just a generation before and now their children and grandchildren forged new careers in city government, civil service and private industry. They were considered successful by most standards. The hamlets strewn across the south shore of the Island still brought a few families from Southern Europe, but these days, more "immigrated" from the lower Eastside and Brooklyn.

Santina was witness to the changes that came with each decade. In the thirties, the Island had the same identity that came with the turn of the century, while the forties brought farewells as husbands, sons – aunts and uncles left for military service. In the sixties, Santina had witnessed that same emotional void as the boys left and returned from Vietnam and other foreign ports.

"Too many boys from the Island have died," Vito would complain. He had been exempt from service due to his age and the fact that he was a father.

"I know, Vito…our Italian boys love this country and many have given their lives," Santina would try to explain and console him.

War quickly changed the complexion of these first immigrant Italian families. They had come to America to escape the hostilities and vile criminal engagement on their own foreign shores. One by one…almost daily, during the heated times of conflict, the STATEN ISLAND ADVANCE would list the names of those who died in battle. When the death notices appeared in the obituary column, people would ask Santina, "Did you know the boy?" With pride and sadness, she would reply.

"Did I know the boy? Yes, I knew them all. They delivered my paper, carried my groceries…dated my daughters and waved to me on the street." The Seamstress felt she was part of the Island's greater community.

In 1939 Santina's family experienced a different kind of death… the kind that is often too difficult to bear. They had rented their middle apartment to a Greek family. It was unusual for the Greeks to find apartments with the Italians. The Greeks stayed to themselves and enjoyed their rich culture and heritage.

The husband came from Argos and found employment with Vito's small company. He allowed his worker to fix up a small area in the company warehouse where he could live. One day the painter announced he wanted to bring his family to America, but would need a bigger place for them when they arrived.

That same evening Santina invited their Greek painter over for dinner and during the discussion he lifted several pictures from an envelope he had received in a letter a few days before. She looked at a photo of his family and told Vito to help him with the expenses to bring the family to America.

Over dinner, on the first night of their arrival, Santina fell in love with their little girl and was able to converse with the mother with her own limited knowledge of the language. They lived with them for over two years and were on their way to saving for a down payment on a house, when on one summer night all their plans went up in smoke. Little Georgia, their only child, who had just celebrated her seventh birthday, was riding her bike when a car ran into her and killed her instantly. The mourning period would not end for either family and sorrow pervaded the entire household for months.

"Vito, we go back to Grrreece!" Nicholas Demopolis announced as he picked up his check on one Friday afternoon.

"What are you talking about, Nick?" Vito asked in surprise.

"My wife, Athena…she wants to go back to her family. My Georgia is gone and we have nothing," he said sorrowfully.

"Have we offended you, Nicky?" Vito asked.

"No! You and your Santina are good people. If not for you, we would be back in Grrreece, months ago," he announced.

"You stay here! You work for me and you live in my house. We are your family. You will have more children," Vito pleaded with him.

Vito shared his conversation with Santina and that night, called up the stairs for the couple to come down for coffee. A few minutes later they appeared through the glass of the dining room door. Vito separated the pocket doors and bade them to enter.

"Athena, how are doing?" Santina asked with all the concern and care within her. The woman looked at her and began to cry helplessly. Santina embraced and kissed her forehead.

"You are not a tenant…you are my sister…my adopted sister and I will not let you go back to Greece. We need you here! Vito needs your husband and I need you…my precious friend.

Three hours passed and a peace began to fill the room. The couple agreed to stay for a few more months to see if they would feel better and get more established. Vito gave his worker a week off and enough money to go on a vacation upstate at Chestnut Lodge, in the little city of Deposit, New York. The Fortunato family vacationed there often. They sent a postcard stating that they were having a good time. Actually, they were having a real good time because nine months later Arianna was born. Good times followed them and their family expanded to include: Alexandria, Thomas, Petros and twins, Santo and Vito – named after you know who!

For the Italians, children defined their future...the basis of their acceptance and stability ten or twenty years down the road. Contraception was forbidden by the church and few, if any, of these faithful Italian-Catholic stalwarts sinned against the edicts of their church. When you were married for six months, people in the community didn't ask you how things were going. The old men would ask, "Did you maka baby?" Six months meant you were old married people and needed to get on with the main purpose of marriage...having children.

When Santina was pregnant, so were her sisters-in-law, her seamstress friends and almost everyone her age. And the babies came late too! Not late in the gestation, but in the age of their mother. It was not uncommon for women to have babies well into the fourth decade of their lives. Big families evolved slowly and methodically. A man married a neighborhood woman...they had children and the children had children. There were babies, babies everywhere!

Santina's children were part of a great community of other "Italian Americans." The second and third generations of offspring were to benefit from college and professional training. They were to move beyond the curbside fruit stands and common labor to positions of leadership and wealth.

But Santina worried about the changes she saw in the children who were supposed to transcend the lowly station of her parents. She saw a new religion emerging...a religion that was taking the place of Catholicism and a strange kind of social ideology that was shaped in humanism and self. This was troubling because the values that shaped her conscience and the fiber of the Italian community were being lost in beliefs that lessened the sanctity of life and permitted everything and anything, as long as it felt good. Santina pondered if a generation or two down the road would have any moral conscience.

She remembered the night her neighbor came to the door and begged to speak to her.

"My daughter....she getta pregnant and sheesa notta married. Where do I go, Santina? Where do I taka her?" she begged.

"What do you mean, signora?" Santina questioned.

"She needs to get fixed," came the answer.

"I don't know what you mean...."fixed?" Santina asked again.

"Abortiona!" she called out.

Here was a Catholic...bound by the rules of the church for all other aspects of her life. She was faithful to attend Mass and would go hungry on Friday night if she had no fish to eat. The real things that accounted for a religious conscience were not enough to support her faith in the greater struggles and problems.

This woman wanted to abort a baby...to kill a child, thought Santina and she must encourage her not to take this life.

"No...she must have the baby and you must help her," Santina pleaded.

"The boy is gone...he goes in the Army. He leaves my daughter and tells her to do this thing," the frightened mother explained.

A few hours later, her daughter also came to the house and listened as Santina pleaded with them not to abort the child. As the years passed, Santina had heard of many abortions and vowed she would do everything to stop it if such an act ever came to her home. Her own girls had not experienced this kind of thing. Perhaps it was Vito, who challenged them to be *clean*, then added that he would kill them if they ever showed up pregnant. This was their belief and no one was going to intimidate them to think otherwise because they would have to answer to papa.

Eight months later a baby boy was born. The girl met a fine man, who adopted the child and things worked out for them. Santina considered the matter one of her great successes in life. Indeed, this is why she was placed on the earth...to give...to help people and preserve life. It was a fond memory...one she thought of each time she looked into the eyes of a newborn. The Seamstress also knew the face and eyes revealed the soul of person. Yes, the eyes declared the very essence of their life.

Never was there a time when a room was filled with people, that Santina didn't see humanity in their faces. She could critique their expressions and read their lives as if they had written every moment for the world to see. The Seamstress looked beyond their wrinkles, their color and age and saw the person as part of a greater civilization...one not shielded from sorrow, anger and bitterness. She thought that expressions...the permanent ones were born in the experiences of one's life. While some individuals thought they could hide their passions within the boundaries of a smile, most could not hold the façade for long. Even the best *actors* had a story to tell... one that flesh could not screen from the rest of the world.

Such was the case with a particular woman whom Santina came to know. She called herself Olga Helm, but that was only a pseudonym for her real name, *Naomi Heimmer.*

She came from Germany to America aboard an ocean liner with her father and mother. While most trips were uneventful, hers would be listed in the history books and she herself, would be part of a miraculous story of courage and fortitude.

Olga left her native country by train and embarked on a cross continent rail ride. The excitement of living in a new world...with new friends was frightening, but her own country was now occupied by the persecutor and tyrant the world had come to know as the Fuehrer...Adolph Hitler. Months before she left the small village near Munich, her parents came face to face with death. They escaped through an underground resistance organization.

It wasn't that they had done something wrong. No! Her parents were good citizens and her father had a good job as a baker. By all accounts, her family was part of the stock of an intelligent and industrialized society. They had done nothing wrong to seek their own exile and faced no jury who would judge them unworthy of their birthright to live where they chose. Their only sin was that they were Jews and would not be permitted to stay in the land their ancestors had chosen many years before.

The train ride was uneventful, except for the sights of lush forests and snow-capped mountains. They reached England and boarded a ship heading for the United States. On their journey, the ships large diesel engines became engulfed in flames when a torpedo struck the bow of the vessel. The great iron basin headed for the deep in the middle of the Atlantic Ocean. There were only a few survivors...one was an eight year old girl.

The Seamstress came to know her through her work at the shop. She was only a young woman when she met Santina on the Staten Island Ferry. Ironically, she was holding a singular employment ad for work as an operator at a small shop in the garment district. The *small shop* was owned by the Neurembergs.

She escorted the frightened girl into the office and Isadore immediately hired her and assigned a sewing machine. Santina kept an eye on the newcomer and they became friends over a period of a few months. Then one day, Santina announced she was leaving the shop. At the same time, Olga took an apartment in Dongan Hills.

As the years went by the two women lost regular contact, but did stay in touch from time to time. Santina marveled at the events the young girl faced as she left Germany...boarding a tanker and experiencing the sea and perils of war. She would go through life with only the memory of her parents. No matter what was said in her presence...a joke or a story, she would smile then would withdraw to the sorrow that nestled deep within her. The Jews had paid an awful price for being who they were and the flight of a simple baker's family was testimony to the cruelty and inhumanity that existed in the souls of men and women.

A half century later...a remnant of the great Holocaust lived quietly in a city far from the land of her birth. She once told Santina that she hated her *German* name, but felt she must bear the marks of her family's flight and keep the memory of what they had suffered. Santina often thought of this kind of human mental torture and could do nothing but pray.

But others faced similar perils and somehow were able to transcend the memory and pain. Adeline's family originally came from Florence. There in the beautiful city, her ancestors had carved out a rich identity...in culture and wealth. If it had not been for a terrible fire, she, like her mother, would have been born in an ancient mansion with servants and maids waiting on her. She might have gone on to one of the best universities in Europe and become a doctor. For sure, Adeline would have been born into the unique brand of wealth known only to the great landowners and industrialists of Italy.

When Santina first met Adeline's mother, she would sit for hours and listen to her stories. The gracious woman spoke of the fashions and great dinner parties she witnessed in her youth. Her memory was sharp and she recalled, with delight, the splendor of her town and mansion.

Then one night, her entire family was trapped in the flames and smoke-filled rooms of their great estate. Only she escaped because she was on holiday in Switzerland with her aunt. A few weeks later, she returned to view the rubble of an edifice that had been built a thousand years before and had been the home of her ancestors. Now she was an orphan and found herself looking for a home. Her aunt made arrangements for her to be sent to a local convent and never again did she live in such splendor. At nineteen she ventured out to find employment.

She began working at a bank in Venice and through a series of events found herself in New York City at an investment convention. There she met Salvatore Lepore, became engaged and never returned to her native land. Santina remembered the passion with which she spoke and the strength shown each time there was mention of her family.

Zia, as Santina called her, was a woman of great joy and reminded her how to laugh and sing and view things in life as mere pebbles... rolling on the sands of a beach.

"You cannot change the events in your life...you can only ask God to lead the way through them," she would share with her adopted niece.

Santina loved being in her presence and made sure her children met her and spent time listening.

"Signora, I will write your story, someday," Santina would tell her.

"My story is nothing, Santina!" she would reply.

"But you braved so much...you lost so much," she would answer the dowager.

"Santina, you cannot lose something that is only borrowed for a moment in time. I was not to be rich or famous. I was to be the wife of an American boy. That is my story and if it is a story of survival...then I survived. We are placed on this earth only to serve others. When you have done this...you have served yourself," was her eloquent reply.

Now, many years later, she would sometimes think of the two women. Poor Olga's fondest memory was tainted by fate and Adeline's mother, who taught others how to survive their fate.

Yes, life was about surviving, and perhaps that is what life was all about...survival. It meant that luxuries were relative to the era and time of one's existence and the real measure of a person was their legacy...the thing they gave or left while spending a life time of singular days in the act of just that...surviving.

"And what are you thinking with such a face on your face?" questioned Carmella.

"Oh, I was just thinking how wonderful my four girlfriends have been to me and how much I love them," she smiled and clutched her hand.

"Would you still love us if we had told Julius that you were the one who called his wife when he started flirting with the girl in Tennanbaum's shop," Carmella teased.

"Do you remember that? Oh, I haven't thought about it in years," replied Santina.

"He should have only known how much we all ratted on him during those years," Antoinette chimed.

Oh, those years? How many were there? It was hard to believe that a lifetime of memories could be found in just a small passage of time of working together.

That's all they were...fleeting, youthful years. Why hadn't they forgotten the little events that filled the days, months and then years? What was it that brought them back time after time to laugh and joke about the brothers, the old shop and the "regulars" who came through the doors?

The girls conceded they would not want to re-live those years, but would not want to have lived without them.

It was Josephina who suggested that they return to the store on the thirtieth anniversary of their last working day. By public transportation, they retraced their steps back to the shop. As they left the cab each stretched their neck to look up at the large window that once was their only view of the world for those long nine and ten hour days.

They imagined that a millinery shop would be there...or some other related industry, but a large, gray painted, plywood board covered most of the window, which was now shattered.

"Look, you can still see part of the name," Carmella called out. There were the remaining letters of the firm's name... "NEUREM." They all gazed in silence and disbelief. The business was gone, the brothers were gone and they were gone too! They had outlived the shop and the Neurembergs. And more...they had outlived the industry, which was now in the remotest parts of the world. Were there other girls sitting in front of sewing machines...dreaming of tomorrow and the promise of a husband or family? They had no doubt.

"Let's go inside," Carmella pleaded.

"Oh, it's too dangerous, Mella," replied Adeline.

"Look...there are birds up in our room," Carmella noticed.

There they were...the city's relentless flying citizens had found their way into the confines of the old work room.

"You go, Santina...you're the bravest!" Adeline called out.

"No, I can't..." she replied.

"Yes, Santina...you go for us and see if it is safe," Antoinette asked in agreement.

Santina made her way to the door and pushed it open. The lock, which was fastened by two rusty nails, fell to her feet and she looked down to see the mosaic tiles lifting from the outer flooring. She remembered the little tiles...neatly placed and once, immovable. Now they testified to the neglect and flooding which made its way up the curb and into the doorway. She pushed the door further and found that debris from the ceiling, including the old wall lamps, had fallen to the ground just behind it.

The Seamstress stepped lightly as she lifted her foot to engage the first step. She teetered back and forth to see if it was strong enough to hold her weight. Back in the old days, her one hundred eighteen pound frame made little burden for these same steps and she remembered how little Carmella would run up the stairs ahead of them in the morning and hop down them in the evening.

Now, at one hundred and sixty pounds, she moved cautiously, step by step, with thoughts only of her safety. Finally, reaching the top, her eyes began to scan the rooms...first quickly, then slowing down to make the conscious comparisons from their original state.

She began to walk around the room and assess its safety for the girls to join her. She looked at the little tables, which still had some sewing machines attached to them. She walked to her own desk and slowly ran her fingers over her Singer, then blowing the dust from the top she saw the little spot where she would rest her gum when she grew tired of chewing. She could see a small place where the lacquer finish was worn and smiled as she visualized the little wad of gum resting in its designated spot.

She opened the door and pushed the contents around with a pen from her purse. In disbelief, she saw a little Bible given to her by the Chinese lady who cleaned the offices and remembered the day the little woman presented it to her.

"Good for you...this good for you mind," she said as she placed the little testament in Santina's hands when she passed by her work station one day. The Seamstress could boast no great hours reading the scriptures while at work, but never removed it from her little desk drawer. There it was...after all these years. She lifted it, wrapped it in some tissue and placed it in one of the side pockets of her purse. It had stayed clean in the sanctuary of the little desk all of these years, she thought, and now deserved a better resting place.

She walked over to the main office where the brothers had literally lived year after year...and *literally* meant exactly that at times.

It was in the middle of winter, when Harry took up residence in there.

"You can't stay here at night...we can't afford the heating bill," Isadore complained.

"So...I'll turn on the heat!" Harry fired back.

"It's twenty degrees outside and ten inside," Isadore yelled.

"So, I'll freeze to death...who cares," Harry answered.

"Who cares? Who cares? You'll die here and the papers will read: BROTHER FREEZES BROTHER TO DEATH!" Isadore shouted.

Harry did stay for a while. Actually, he stayed until April, when his wife finally let him back in the house. His playful antics cost him some cold nights, but still, he never took his eyes off of the ladies.

Santina walked to their desks and thought they appeared so much bigger and more imposing back in the old days. Now they were dust ridden antiques of the past...her past and that of the girls. There was something depressing about the room and she began to feel anxious. The reality of these vacant years left their mark on the upper quarters of this building with rotting floors, decaying and falling ceilings and rusty metal on the heating units. She turned to see a pigeon empty itself on some old bolts of cloth near the window. The mildew began to overtake her senses and she made her way down the stairs.

She felt depressed and disappointed. Wasn't the world of her youth supposed to remain as it had been so many years ago? Knowing the girls, her first thought was to protect them from the eerie confines of the rooms and not tell them about the lack of solid flooring, the rust, decay and rubble strewn throughout the room.

"How is it?" Carmella cried out, almost enthusiastically.

"It is," Santina paused and studied their faces. "It...it is not safe for all of us to see it together." It is nothing like you remember...just an empty room," She lied to protect their memory.

Santina looked at her friends and confessed. "It's completely ruined...dirty and smelly. Keep your memories and let's go."

For some reason, no one contested or complained as they clutched each other's hands and made their way down the street. Three years later, Santina had occasion to drive with her daughter into Manhattan. They drove by the old building and noted that fire had gutted it out completely and only a few walls and the concrete basement remained.

The *Shoppe* was gone...now it was only a memory and not to be brooded over. Santina looked back as the car made its way around the corner. As she made her last sight of the structure, she whispered, "Good bye."

"Whoya you talking to, Grandma?" Her granddaughter questioned.

"Oh...just someone I once knew...many years ago, darling!" she answered, and then clutched the child lovingly.

"Santina...Santina!" A voice called from the entrance door.

Standing at the doorway, late as usual, was Giovanni Pennini, one of her husband's faithful employees. She hadn't seen him in years. Standing next to him was his wife, Alberta. They both smiled as they made their way over to her.

Giovanni had changed little over the years. He bore the same smile and sturdy frame. She and Vito had sponsored Giovanni when he first came from the Island of Corsica. He was supposed to be distantly related to Vito, but they could find no common ancestry. Still, he had a strange likeness to Vito and people often confused them for brothers. He was a young man of strong character. He met Alberta at a dance sponsored by the YMCA on Richmond Terrace and he fell head over heels for her. Such was not the case with Alberta. She was more infatuated with a young sailor who was stationed in Red Hook, over in Brooklyn. She would board the ferry and bus to see him every weekend. During the sixteen months, they had become intimate and spoke of plans to marry. Then one day, without any warning, he disappeared. When she went to the rooming house to see him, the landlord could not attach the name she gave to any tenant. The soldier had not only lied, but did something else...he left her pregnant as well.

Giovanni came one night to speak to Vito. He had often come by the house to seek Vito's advice on personal matters; but that night it was different. They went to the living room and spent several hours together. The big question to be answered was whether he should ask Alberta to marry...knowing she was pregnant by another man.

"Do you love this girl?" Vito asked.

"Si....ah, yes, Vito!" the youth replied.

"I cannot answer for you," Vito said as he turned to pour a glass of wine, and then asked, "Did you speak to the priest?"

"Yes," he answered

"And what did he say?" Vito asked.

"He said to ask my father!" he replied.

"And I'm your father?" Vito smiled.

"You are all I have in this country...the only one I can ask," he answered.

"Let me ask you. If Alberta was to move back to Italy, what would you do?" Vito asked

"I would save enough money to move to her," he replied.

"Why do you ask me if you should marry her? You have already answered your own question," Vito summed, then smiled.

"Tomorrow, I will ask her father," Giovanni resigned.

"Did you ask her?" Vito questioned.

"No!" he answered.

"NO! You want to marry a girl and you haven't asked her yet," Vito cried out.

"I will ask her...but first, I must ask her father," he answered.

Two months later, Vito and Santina made all the necessary plans for a wedding and reception...at a Chinese Restaurant. The girl's parents were immigrants and had no money, so Vito and Santina spent three hundred dollars of their own money and married off the two. A few months later, they moved to Philadelphia and he began work on several housing developments. Fifteen years later, they found themselves back on Staten Island in a small house in the remote section called Huguenot. Now, thirty years later, six children and three grandchildren, they were still married and the look on their faces told that they had successfully bridged those early years together and the struggles of raising a family.

"Santina...Santina!" He called as he neared and reached to hug her. When the kisses and hugging ended, they exchanged greetings and updated each other on their children.

"Thank you for saving my life," Alberta whispered in Santina's ear.

"We did what we thought was right for the both of you," Santina repeated lovingly.

Thank you for saving my life! Oh, how she wished a little advice and three hundred dollars could save other lives. In one case, it took much more and the results were not the same.

His name was Sammy, the son of Enzo Cuggiani, who worked for Vito. His wife had died and he was a single parent to his only son. His lack of time and parenting skills took its toll on the boy.

As early as his first day in kindergarten, his teacher reported that Sammy couldn't keep his hands to himself. Seventeen years later, he still couldn't keep his hands to himself...and was accused of striking and seriously wounding an off-duty police officer in a local bar. A lack of witnesses made the city's case weak and his bail was set at fifty thousand dollars...necessitating ten percent in cash...upfront! Three days after the crime was committed, Enzo pleaded his case with Vito and Santina. Something told them not to put up the money, but they saw the desperation of their countryman and yielded.

Five thousand dollars was all they had in their business and personal account, but they pledged it for the bail. Enzo promised to pay it off by working extra hours for Vito and doing other odd jobs during the next few years. Three weeks later the boy jumped bail and headed for Mexico. When the police extradited him back to the States, he forcibly took a gun and killed one of them. He was sent to prison and while awaiting trial, was thrown from the third floor of the prison facility to his death. After all those years he still couldn't keep his hands to himself! As for Enzo, he died sixteen months later from a massive heart attack. Sometimes you pay a big price for helping others.

Vito and Santina avoided the topic and rarely spoke of the incident. As always, they did what they thought was right and were ready to pay a price for it...and this time they certainly did.

Over the years the couple had invested money in others and never questioned their motives. They had committed themselves to helping people and their only motivation was one of giving.

And while their help was appreciated by most, there were those times when they were sorry they *got involved*. Such was the case with Mario Carbonaro.

When he appeared at their door at three in the morning, he was dressed only in his shorts. The couple scrambled to get him in the house and out of the ten degree temperatures that frosted the air.

"She threw me out!" he explained as Santina placed a blanket around his body.

"Why?" Vito asked.

"Don't ask!" He answered.

"Don't ask? Don't ask? You come to my house in the middle of the night and tell me, don't ask?" Vito complained.

"Okay...it's a long story," Mario began.

"Shorten it...it's three in the morning and I have to get up for work, capisce?" Vito fired back.

"I met somebody at work and Vivian found out about it," he continued.

"So...Vivian threw you out!" Santina offered.

"No...my mother!" Mario answered.

"So Sarina did the job to you," laughed Vito.

"Yeah! And there's more," the playboy answered.

"More?" questioned Vito.

"Yeah...all of my clothing is on the front lawn as we speak and they expect snow tonight," Mario answered.

Vito rose and pulled his neighbor by the arm and led him to the bedroom where he tossed some clothing into his arms. Ten minutes later they ran down the street, gathered the clothing and brought it back to Vito's basement. Santina had already placed some fresh bedding on the couch and within minutes, Mario was fast asleep.

"The dope!" Vito exclaimed as he lay next to Santina in their bed a few minutes later.

"What do we do?" she asked.

"We get Vivian over the house and try to help them through this mess," Vito stated, disgusted.

But the calamity was yet to come! The couple did meet and went back to their apartment. It was less then a month later when his mother, Sarina, appeared at their door in fright and confusion.

"She'll kill him! My daughter-in-law will kill him!" she cried out as she threw open the back porch door leading to Santina's kitchen.

"You go Vito," Santina called to her husband.

"Yes, they will only listen to you, Vito," Sarina begged.

"Me...why me?" Vito responded.

Ten minutes later, he climbed the steps to their little apartment and he pushed the door open. Amidst broken glass and shattered dishes, Vito found Mario barricaded behind the kitchen table.

"She's crazy, Vito...crazy!" Mario cried out.

"I'll kill the bast..." Vivan angrily called out, but Vito interrupted her.

"He's your husband...you can't kill your husband! Stop...stop it now!" Vito demanded.

Perhaps it was fatigue or time to call it quits, but Vivian threw down the last dish and began to cry. A moment later, Santina appeared at the door, walked over and took the weeping girl in her arms. Five hours later and two pots of coffee they agreed to call a truce for the night.

Within a month, they were back together as they had been before. But there was a catch! Sarina was angry that Vito was able to get them back together.

"He's no good...no good. My husband Enzo...his own father knew he was no good...I didn't listen...Vivian didn't listen...he's no good! My own son is no good! If my Enzo was alive, he would kill him," she screamed.

That night in bed, Vito turned to his wife and questioned.

"You help people...you make people angry! Ah! I don't know what to do. Maybe next time, I mind my own business and you mind my own business too," he complained.

"Vito, you did what you had to do! Go to bed!" she answered as she quickly dozed into her slumber.

"Yes, I did what I had to do and now Sarina is angry. I don't know what to do!" he spoke as his wife dozed next to him.

"Ah...she sleeps and I worry," he spoke as he clicked out the light and found his own rest minutes later.

Of all the things in Santina's life for which she was grateful, Vito was at the top of the list. Never was there a time that she questioned his integrity; and there were times they went without, rather than compromise their standards.

It was in the summer of '52 when Simon Martin, one of his big customers came to their door and requested a favor.

"Vito, I need your help!" he began.

"Anything, Mr. Martin...anything!" Vito replied.

"Good...because I need a big favor. First, let me thank you for the wonderful job you did on my building.

"Thank you, Mr. Martin. I'm all ready to start on the building next to it. We should have the new electric in the entire building in about a month." Vito replied.

"Well, that's what I'm here to talk to you about. You see, the city would like to purchase my two buildings. They want to tear them down and build a police station. Now...here's where you come in. They are about to make their offer and they'll pay me for any work or repairs I did on them in the last two years. If you'll just write a bill for putting new electric in both buildings, I can get more money out of them. Of course, I'll give you some money for doing this." Martin explained.

"This...this is a lie and I cannot do it. I'm sorry, Mr. Martin."

"Sorry, sorry? You people are all alike...with your high and mighty morals," Martin shot back in disgust, but Vito countered.

"Mr. Martin, four months ago my men put new electric wire in your building. When you ordered the job, you said you wanted the best and I gave you the best. The wire is inside the walls and you would have never known if I used the cheaper wire. You paid for the best, I gave you the best. I did not cheat you and I would never cheat my customers. Please, Mr. Martin...please do not ask me to do this thing. Good night!" Vito finished and watched as his customer stood speechless in the dark.

He closed the door, turned and found his Santina with her arms open and a big smile on her face.

"Vito, you are still the man I married...never changing...honest and beautiful," she called to him.

The two embraced, turned and went to bed. As for his customer, he never again used Vito's company for construction or repairs. Interestingly, *Mr. Bancroft C. Martin III* was on the cover of the *ADVANCE* a few years later for nothing less then tax evasion.

"Life should be very simple!" Santina would tell her children. "You do the right thing and you are blessed. Your father and I had very little, but had everything we needed to make us happy. At night, I would move my foot to touch your father's foot and my world was complete. To me he was everything! I trusted him and he loved me...what more could a woman want or need. Keep your life simple, my children."

Their love and trust was something that everyone admired and some felt, had a strange power in and of itself. That *strange power* demonstrated itself in a most unusual way on a cold February night in 1959. They were given tickets to see a show in a small play house on 42nd street in Manhattan's theater district. They ventured in on the Ferry and subway, arriving just a few blocks from their destination. It was when they were leaving the theater, that a man came up behind the couple and ordered them to keep walking down the street. Vito was sure that a gun of some sort was nestled close to his spine. Finally, they came to an opening in one of the store fronts a few blocks from Broadway.

"I have a few dollars...all I ask is that you don't hurt my wife. Let me reach for my wallet and I'll give you the money," Vito pleaded with the man.

"Okay, but move slowly...I've got the gun on your woman," came the response.

Vito slowly reached for his wallet, thinking Santina was also going to cooperate. That was not to be the case because the brave seamstress turned to her attacker and ordered, "You turn around and leave us alone!" she ordered. Then, as if a miracle had occurred, he turned and ran down the street.

Vito stood, more in amazement than shock.

"Are you crazy? He could have hurt you," Vito barked.

"I was not worried about him hurting me...I was worried he would hurt you and if he did...who would finish painting the dining room walls for the party on Friday night...who?" Santina called back to him.

There were other times when their love proved to be stronger than some of life's obstacles. It happened that Vito had purchased all the necessary supplies for an extension on a customer's house. The materials were delivered to the sight and were stolen during the night. Six thousand dollars in supplies and materials were gone and Vito was responsible for them.

"What do I do?" Vito questioned Santina over dinner.

"It is a matter of what shall...WE do?" she answered.

The two gazed into each other's eyes and Santina spoke.

"I will take in some altering and make some wedding dresses."

"No!" he complained.

"Yes...and we will not speak about it again," she ordered.

Three years later, working late into the evening, Santina and Vito cleared their debt at the bank for the materials. But their unexpected reward was yet to come.

During the years, Vito Fortunato had always made his services free to the older men and women in the neighborhood. If they needed a repair, he would send one of his men to look into the work. Looking into the work usually meant picking up the bill as well. A few weeks after they paid off their bank note, Santina called Vito at work to let him know a certified letter came to their door via a special courier. It was a letter from a Staten Island lawyer petitioning Vito to come to his office for matters pertaining to a certain client.

The last will and testament of their neighbor, Mrs. Eloise Lancaster was to be read at a lawyer's office on Forest Avenue at two o'clock on Friday. Vito took the afternoon off from work and together they made their way to the office for the reading of the will. To their amazement, the old woman had left them one of her properties...an old house on Bard Avenue. They were given the keys to the house and drove out to see it that night.

Within a few weeks, Vito's men renovated it and a tenant signed a two-year lease on the house. Then two years later she signed another and ten years later she was still signing two-year leases.

The most fascinating thing about the whole affair is that while Vito had completed many little jobs for the widow, he had only met her face-to-face...one time.

Little did they realize that to others their kindness and generosity seemed to have no end!

When Josephina's mother needed an operation or when her cousin Aldo and his wife Lisa needed a down payment on a house, it was Santina and Vito who happened to have a "few extra dollars in the bank," they would loan with no demands for repayment.

At night, in bed, the generous couple would share their joy in helping others and when Vito died, hundreds of family and friends came to the funeral and told their story of our they were helped by the couple.

It seemed from that point on, the funerals came in succession. First Vito, then Santina's brothers and sisters passed. Where the marriage ceremony dominated the social events in their early years, the "funeral" had replaced it in the latter years.

Angelina Caruso's wake was just a link in the long chain of funerals processions.

"So girls, when do we leave," Carmella asked excitedly.

"Carmella, you're supposed to sit and be quiet," Adeline reprimanded her.

"Oh, she's dead and I'm hungry," Carmella answered.

"Shh!" Josephina motioned to the quarreling girls.

"We will go in just minute, girls," Santina called to them.

Across the room, more and more people were leaving. They would walk to the front row, greet family members they hardly knew or had never met, then walk through the large doors and disappear into the hallway. The girls watched as the rest of the remaining mourners filed by the family and made their way to the parking lot.

"Santina...you need a ride?" called a voice.

"We all need a ride! My husband dropped us off and I was going to call him to come and get us," Antoinette answered.

"Don't bother, I'll take you all home," came the reply.

Johnny Marconi was a neighborhood kid who played in the streets with Santina's boys. He was a gentle kid who never married.

"Johnny, we are going to Ten Bows...wanna come?" Carmella asked.

"Chinks? You bet," he answered.

"Well, let's get our coats and hats," said Santina, as she began to rise.

"Sit right back down, Snookie, I've got a few things to tell you about last Wednesday night," came a voice from behind her.

It was Maria LaBella, Santina's Bingo partner at St. Mary's in Rosebank. Maria's husband worked for Vito for a few months when he was laid off from his job. Vito employed him as a plumber's helper...that is until his master plumber started screaming at one of the job sites and the men made a nervous call to their boss for help.

"I'm gonna killa him! I aska for a wrencha, he givva me a hamm! I aska for fluxa, he giva me a wrencha! I don't know whatta to do? Vito you gotta getta him witha somebody else!"

"Patience, Carmine! Tomorrow, I'll put him with Ralph DeMarco," he promised.

That was many years ago and a few dozen funerals before the one they were now attending.

"Did you see that witch...she cheated...I know she did," Maria began.

"What witch?" Santina questioned.

"MARGARET FLYNN!" She cried out.

"How do you cheat at Bingo," Antoinette called out.

"She cheats! She's in cahoots with the caller. She says she has the number, but she doesn't. And when she goes up to check the numbers, I know he cheats for her," Maria finished.

"She thinks everybody cheats," Santina whispered to the girls. For nearly sixteen years, Santina and Maria went to the church on Wednesdays. Sometimes they would eat dinner at Bacci's Hamburger Haven on Hylan Blvd and skip Bingo and go to a movie. Those nights had their "outstanding memories" too. One night, they were at a restaurant and witnessed a hold up. They were sitting and eating when a man entered the restaurant.

"That's a catch!" stated Maria.

"Who?" asked Santina.

"The gun over there with the guy....I mean the guy over there with the...ggggun!" answered Maria, raising her voice as she spoke.

"GUN!" She screamed so loud that all of the patrons rose to their feet. Then the chaos began. People started running and screaming. The would be hold-up man ran out of the restaurant and when the manager pieced the events of the evening together, he concluded that Maria had saved the day! He handed her a fifty dollar bill and promised dinner on the house the following Wednesday.

A moment later, Santina and the girls were at the clothing rack pulling their coats off their hangers. But Carmella couldn't find her coat. In its place was a fake fur, which had replaced her real mink. They called the funeral director immediately and he went into a song and dance about his liability. The girls searched the entire funeral parlor together.

Just as they began to give up hope of finding it, Santina's cousin, Graziella's younger son, Ralph appeared with the coat.

"I think my mother took this by accident. Please excuse us," he said as he presented the coat to Santina and turned to walk away.

"I think your mother will need this," Carmella said as she handed Ralph his mother's coat.

"She knew what she was doing!" Antoinette said angrily, as the boy had disappeared into the foyer. None of the girls countered her as they all knew about Cousin Graziella! She had been in the habit of "borrowing" things from people for years. Once, when Santina visited her house, she saw her mother's entire Chinese tea set nestled on the lower shelf of her breakfront. The family thief must have taken one piece at time, because no one ever noticed it was gone. Santina would never dream of taking it back. Her mother had told her years before that her cousin was a collector of anything that wasn't nailed down!

Oh, the stories Santina could tell about her family...the cousins, uncles, aunts and the *borrowers*.

"Well girls, we have our coats and hats...time to go," Santina smiled. They made their way to the foyer, with Johnny Marconi leading the way.

"I'll pull the car around," he called to the girls.

As they moved to the doorway, Bradianna, the daughter-in-law of the dead, approached them and spoke.

"Ladies, thank you for coming. My darling mother loved you all and spoke of you often."

"We loved her too," Santina said, as the two grasped hands. "How is your husband taking it?" Josephina asked.

"He's been all broken up. But he knew she was sick and now she no longer sick," came Bradianna's answer.

"Tell your husband Tommy, we are thinking about him. If you need us, you know you can call...anytime...for anything," said Antoinette.

"Thank you and good night!" she replied as she kissed each of them respectfully.

"Come...the car is waiting," Johnny called.

The girls made their way down the steps and exited the building.

"She's a beautiful girl," commented Carmella endearingly as she eyed the girl and blew a kiss through the entrance door window.

The kiss was an important part of the social protocol of the Italian community. A kiss was the endearing token of love and affection among family members and friends.

When Tony Caccese didn't kiss his mother as she leaned over to him at church, his father could be heard saying, "Just you wait until you get home." There would be another sermon delivered by his father when he stepped into the house.

Not to kiss a loved one in public was an act of disrespect and such an act did not go un-noticed or unchecked. The boy never again veered away from his mother when she went to kiss him. Such affection was inherent to many immigrant communities and respectful acts were a part of the total social clime. If you saw your aunt, you kissed her. Should you be walking down the street and come upon your mother's best friend...you kissed her. If you didn't, the entire community would be buzzing and your buttocks might be too when you got home.

Various acts of respect were expected from a "countryman." The men even kissed. For the men, the station of *paesano* was one of ancestry and identity. There were actions of respect that sometimes, if not expressed, cost a person embarrassment...while other times, more severe forms of shunning and even death. Few would ever forget Giuseppe Camardi, Vito's cousin, who never learned his place in the community.

As a boy, he found adjustment to America difficult and fell in with the wrong crowd. One day, just after he turned twenty-one, he showed disrespect to the butcher's wife by calling her some unspeakable words. The butcher jumped over the counter with a knife and performed some unplanned surgery on his abdomen. When the cops arrived, he tried to explain his misfortune by saying he cut himself. But the wounds were too many and the authorities didn't buy his account of what happened. It was only when Santina pleaded with police officials at the hospital to entrust him to her care, did they let him go. A court appearance yielded no findings and the disrespectful youth got off with a reprimand from the judge for being *careless*. For reasons of self-preservation, he would never dare accuse the butcher...that would mean another act of disrespect on top of his last one. No, he would remain silent and move on.

One would think such an incident would cure the average person, but not Giuseppe. Three years later, Santina sat in a courtroom where the judge sentenced the young man to twelve years in prison for brawling and seriously injuring another man. The facts of the case found him, once again, disrespecting and arguing with the man over his daughter's virginity. That was the ultimate disrespect to a father and he should have known better.

The girls gathered into the big *Buick Park Avenue* and the car made its way out into the traffic on the busy street. The funeral was officially over. Within a few days, Santina would call some of the members of the family and offer any help or assistance they might need. For the most part, while there was a great community of Italians that came together for every little occasion, few would allow anyone to invade their privacy or become privy to their family secrets. Should they allow Santina into their home, surely she would leave with a wealth of information. This could not be allowed. What the bereaved did not realize is that every family had them...SECRETS! They were part of being a family.

"So, what are you going to order," Carmella asked the group.

"Chop suey, white rice and mixed vegetables for starters" Josephina answered.

"I wanna try something different," Antoinette added.

"What's different...it's all the same!" Adeline commented.

"When we get there, we'll look at the menu and see if there is something new to try," said Santina in an effort to redirect the conversation. Then turning to the girls she announced solemnly, "Girls, another one of us gone?"

"Yeah, we're getting old!" Carmella added

"You...you're the youngest, the healthiest and the richest," Antoinette commented.

"No, Santina is right. Another one of us is gone...who'll be next?" Josephina said sadly and watched as the girls all grew silent.

"Listen, we can get morbid about this subject or we can get ready for a big dish of chicken chow mien," Santina suggested.

"Santina's right! When it's our time to go...we go!" said Adeline to sum things.

The car moved slowly through traffic onto Bay Street, then turned at Tappen Park and headed down Broad to the restaurant.

As Johnny began to look for a parking space on the busy street, Carmella called out excitedly, "There it is!"

"Don't worry if you have to park far away...we'll walk," Josephina called out.

The car finally settled a few buildings away from the restaurant and the girls made their way to the front door. Upon entering, one could smell the hearty odors of Chinese cooking. While Chinese food was an Italian favorite, there were other *culinary choices* they held sacred. For instance, Christmas Eve was a time for fish of every variety and at Easter the lamb made its way to the table.

Not unlike any other national group, the Italian family table was the conference center for the home. Disputes and announcements found their pulpit in the kitchen or dining room in the evening or on Sunday. If Papa had to lay down a rule...the dinner table served as the bully pulpit. Should someone need to unload a problem, they waited until Sunday lunch.

When Vinny Capriccio, Santina's godson, wanted to tell his parents he had joined the army, he waited until the macaroni was on the plate and the meatballs were being passed. Within seconds, his mother went to pieces and his father grew angry. His older brother came to the rescue.

"Pop...Pop...It's done! Finito," he argued.

With that, his mother grew less teary-eyed and his father called out, "Whattayougonna do?"

That's when the veal cutlets were passed and the wine glasses refilled. Yes, the table was a place to resolve any and all issues and somehow everyone was usually satisfied by the time dessert was served.

"Oh look, there's Father Santo over in the booth," Carmella said excitedly.

"Shh! Carmella, let the man eat in peace!" called Adeline as the girls made their way down the isle, lead by the proprietor.

"You like here?" he respectfully asked as the group flanked a large table in the rear of the restaurant.

"This is fine!" Santina told him.

"That good...I bring menu now," the Chinese waiter announced.

A minute later they began to study column A and column B on the menu in hopes of finding something new to dine on; but when the waiter took their orders, each ordered the same regiment of favorites.

"I love chinks," Carmella said, in a voice too loud.

"Chinese food, Carmella...Chinese food," Santina scolded her.

"Well, we used to say chinks, in the old days" Carmella sarcastically challenged.

"What we used to do and what we should do now are two different things. We need to say Chinese food, okay? Santina answered.

"Well...all right," came, the hesitant reply.

Even now...after so many years, the girls still listened respectfully to their adopted matriarch.

It was about twenty minutes before the food was served and the girls continued their discussions. There was never any pretence or form for their conversations...they talked, usually finding a millisecond of silence and somehow dove in with their opinion or idea. A patron listening to them from a nearby booth, found one wondering if any of the participants heard anything other then their own chatter. Yet, conversation was important...it was necessary and almost coveted by the girls each time they came together. If something happened in their little community, they relied on the information each had gleaned and sorted out the details when they would meet. And of course...they labeled everything and everybody.

When Pasquale D'Amato's wife ran off with another man, she fell under the category of "puttana." Mike Santoro's son, Johnny never worked a day in his life and bore the moniker, "Johnny Mattress." Because Andolina Marino's two boys had an eye for the women, they were both known as "Gigolos." And some were labeled "nutso," as Adeline called them.

It was Santina's distant cousins from the Bronx who took the cake. They would periodically show up for dinner on Sunday all decked out with huge gold earrings, gaudy hats, low cut blouses and clothing three sizes too small for their frames. And the make up…it would be caked on like the frosting on a *napoleon!* Caterina, the elder drew the most laughs from the girls. Her mannerisms were comical and her use, or rather misuse of the English language made her listeners run for cover. To her, it was *versa-visa* and *amonomous.* When asked her dress size, she would respond by saying, "Oh, I'm peteek!" Caterina Zullo was many things…"peteek" was not one of them!

Whether it was a film, movie star, cake mix or a new priest in the local parish, they were women of opinion and offered it, most of the time unsolicited and often offensive.

"Hey, why don't we go and see a show next week. I heard "Sweeney Todd" is wonderful. It's about a barber who eats people!" said Carmella excitedly.

"A barber who eats people? Count me out!" Adeline answered.

"How 'bout going to the Concord for the weekend?" Josephina suggested.

"Maybe we should go to Cape May for the weekend?" Antoinette offered.

Every so often, the five would venture off for a few days and leave their family to catch up on things. Now, with their family raised, they found themselves with time… a lot of time. Chance had brought them together and love kept them together. Each sought to fill the hours and the days with little activities. When Santina called the girls during the week, they would report how busy they were with projects put off for many years. Antoinette spent all of her time sorting her pictures and putting them in albums. She would comment, "When I'm done I'll be ready to die!"

Perhaps that is why it was an ongoing project…one that was well into its second decade.

And worry was an important part of living too! The girls had a list of things that consumed them. When one list was exhausted, they would find something else to be anxious about. Yes, worrying was good too! It kept them alive and focused on their children and grandchildren.

The girls did share one thing! They all had a tremendous sense of right and wrong. They struggled with the changing world and often would sit for hours complaining and critiquing what they liked and loathed.

Above all, they assumed that they must keep their families on the straight and narrow. In their case, the "narrow" was very narrow... with little compromise for the changing morality in the world. Santina learned how to effectively deal with people who married into the family. While the others presumed that their daughters-in-law should listen to their 'pearls of wisdom,' the senior seamstress knew that she must remain a resource should they ever need her. Again, silence was part of her input.

When her daughter-in-law, Victoria, suspected that her husband was getting a little too familiar with a co-worker, it was Santina who confronted him.

"Bobby, how are you doing?" Santina tenderly asked her son one night when he came by for a quick visit and a cup of coffee.

"I'm fine, mom!" he answered.

"If there is ever anything I can do for you, remember to call me," she continued.

"Hey mom...what's this all about?" her son questioned.

"I remember the first night you brought Victoria to meet me. She was beautiful then...aaand she is still beautiful. Five children she gave you and still she looks wonderful. I don't think you could have found a girl who would love you more. Don't you agree?" she asked. Her son stood still for a moment. Santina watched as his eyes began to swell. She moved closer and embraced him. In the next hour he told his story of how he met a woman at work and began a relationship. They had not been intimate, but he didn't know how to break up.

"You say nothing...you just stop engaging her at work. She will not understand any kind of explanation because she is a troubled person. Troubled...because she would do such a thing as try to seduce you! Stay away from her my boy...don't hurt your Victoria." Within a few weeks she met again with her daughter-in-law and the two spent the afternoon shopping. The subject never came up in conversation.

Advice was a part of their daily regiment and whether solicited or not, the five could "advise" you at a moments notice.

"Ah, the food is coming," Carmella announced excitedly.

The waiter distributed the various dishes as the girls continued their chorus of talking. As expected, thirty minutes later they asked for 'doggie bags' for the leftovers.

"I don't eat much anymore," Antoinette announced.

"The same with me," Josephina added.

The five split the bill and moved slowly to the clothing rack, donned their coats and left the restaurant. They walked to the car and in a few moments it entered the traffic on its mission to see that all of its occupants were brought safely home.

First, they took the long ride to drop off Josephina in Great Kills then went on to Carmella's house. Adeline and Antoinette were dropped off together as they were going to spend the night together at Adeline's house. Santina waved as the car continued homeward. The busy day was ending.

In a few minutes Santina Fortunato would be home. She would quickly shower, change to her robe, turn on the television and watch the evening news. She had paid her respects and visited once again with her friends. They would meet again...hopefully soon. No matter how tired they might feel, the little seamstresses always found the strength and time for each other. Santina was amazed at her own strength.

If she was in her seventies, why did she feel so young? It was only the mirror that betrayed her feelings and her grandchildren who remarked while shopping, "Grandma, let me help you with the basket...you're old."

The television news station would report the usual: Someone was murdered, a fire destroyed some old house, the Mayor had an important announcement to make and somewhere in the world, there was war. Santina knew all about these things. One doesn't live a life-time without experiencing the humanity and inhumanity of mankind. She was an eyewitness to a changing world...one that was far, far away from the world she once lived in long ago.

Santina Fortunato started her life with her parents in a cold-water flat, washed laundry by hand in a sink and saw her mother prepare every meal from scratch. Now frozen food dinners, side-by-side refrigerators and automatic dishwashers were paving the way for effortless living and more leisure time. Her mother and father never knew these *wonders* of science and technology, yet their simple life was unencumbered and a generation later...envied. Everywhere Santina looked, something reminded her of the loving couple she called *mamma* and *papa*.

Her breakfront was filled with remnants of her past; things from her mother, aunts and friends. Atop her piano were dozens of pictures of her children and grandchildren. And then there were the favors from the weddings she had attended over the years. Santina reasoned she must have attended a hundred weddings or more. She had seen all of her children marry and she hoped she would be there for the weddings of her grandchildren and great-grandchildren. But she knew that could never be.

Santina was not about to question the events of the past or present. Her days would be filled with doing little things, reflecting and whispering her prayers in the quiet rooms. She would busy herself and not question the day or its fast pace. Anyway, it would disregard her desire for it to be prolonged and follow the Maker's plan, opening and closing accordingly.

Santina would eventually lose control of her affairs and perhaps the other mechanisms that made her independent and useful to her children. Her prayer was that she would never be a burden to them as some of her friends had been to their children. She remembered her friend, Cecilia Ameroso, who died quietly in her sleep, having never suffered a day in her life. That was the way she hoped to leave when her time came.

She poured herself a cup of hot tea and embraced what remained of the evening. Sleep would come easy tonight, as she was tired from the events of the day. In an hour or so, she would check all the windows and locks, then finally retire for the evening.

The other girls would do likewise and most likely have the same thoughts and anxieties. It was part of being old and watching the evening shadows slip over one's world. Each differed, but their age and their living had all brought them to same stage in their lives at the same time. They would all claim to have the stamina and energy to forge ahead cutting and sewing a dress for one of their grandchildren, but Carlo, the tailor would have to "finish" up the work...which was barely started. As they had shared their youth, now their lives would parallel once again...with the activities that they once witnessed with the *old people*.

But their lives had been rich, because they had known a kind of friendship and bond that was not familiar to the youth of the day. Their chance union, made possible by employment in a dingy second floor sewing room, a half century before, was one of the treasures of their lives. They had outlived their other friends and in God's providence, had been given the years to grow old together. No matter how hard or furious was their fight over the ridiculous things that hamper most relationships they never let the day end without a flurry of phone calls to each other. That was the depth of their love for each other and their passion to remain as close as they had been so many years before.

As Santina readied to close the house, she paused at a window and looked out onto the street. She watched as a gentle rain began to fall. The sudden downpour would clean the streets and ready the earth for spring and all of its greening.

She clicked the light and tiptoed to her bedside. Then she pushed her slippers off and lowered her dressing gown onto the rocking chair in the corner. She might have stumbled, but her feet knew the six steps necessary to reach her pillow. She lowered herself onto the bed and pulled the covers over her weary body. Her heart was heavy and she felt a strange quiver in her chest as she folded her hands as if praying.

The day was over and now Santina Fortunato listened to the silence of night. As she lay in bed, her last words were predicable... they were the same words she had prayed night after night...year after year.

"Oh, God," she would begin, "Thank you for this day. If you give me tomorrow, I will give it back to my children and grandchildren. Amen." It was a simple prayer, but told the life and revealed the spirit of this humble Seamstress.

On this night a much different kind of sleep awaited Santina Calabrese Fortunato. While she had obediently yielded her eyes to the darkness, she would not greet the coming day. It was time for her little heart to rest and it chose this hour to stop its life-long vigil. In the morning or sometime during the day, it would be discovered that she had completed her living on this earth.

Throughout her years there were no pretenses from the daughter of Carmine and Lucia and wife of Vito Fortunato. This was a simple and unassuming servant and even obliged death by slipping quietly into eternity.

Santina had lived a beautiful life and would be remembered for her many roles as daughter, wife, mother, sister, grandmother, aunt and friend. She had earned these titles by virtue of living and of course, loving.

In the next few days, notice of her passing would appear in the STATEN ISLAND ADVANCE. The text of her obituary would not have to be composed by a friend or relative, for she had already written and given it to her daughter in a sealed envelope. It included a picture taken a few years before and a short script about her devotion to her husband and family. It also included specific instructions as to how it must be titled - for it was her wish to be remembered as…

SANTINA CALABRESE FORTUNATO
"SEAMSTRESS"

Printed in the United States
77933LV00002B/451-501

9 781600 341106